UNDER FIRE

Clint rode Duke at a gallop and as he topped a rise the shots became much clearer. Looking down he saw that three Conestoga wagons were under siege. They were being circled by mounted men who appeared to be a mixture of whites and Indians—more likely Comancheros, about a dozen of them.

The people in the wagons needed help.

He turned Duke and rode hard for the closer rise. As they approached he drew his rifle from the scabbard and dismounted even before the big gelding had come to a stop.

He threw himself onto the ground and sighted down the barrel of his rifle. His first shot took a man right from his saddle as if he'd been jerked by a rope...

DON'T MISS THESE
ALL-ACTION WESTERN SERIES
FROM THE BERKLEY PUBLISHING GROUP

THE GUNSMITH by J. R. Roberts
Clint Adams was a legend among lawmen, outlaws, and ladies. They called him . . . the Gunsmith.

LONGARM by Tabor Evans
The popular long-running series about U.S. Deputy Marshal Long—his life, his loves, his fight for justice.

LONE STAR by Wesley Ellis
The blazing adventures of Jessica Starbuck and the martial arts master, Ki. Over eight million copies in print

SLOCUM by Jake Logan
Today's longest-running action Western. John Slocum rides a deadly trail of hot blood and cold steel.

ORPHAN TRAIN

J. R. ROBERTS

JOVE BOOKS, NEW YORK

If you purchased this book without a cover, you should be aware that this book is stolen property. It was reported as "unsold and destroyed" to the publisher, and neither the author nor the publisher has received any payment for this "stripped book."

ORPHAN TRAIN

A Jove Book / published by arrangement with
the author

PRINTING HISTORY
Jove edition / October 1994

All rights reserved.
Copyright © 1994 by Robert J. Randisi.
This book may not be reproduced in whole
or in part, by mimeograph or any other means,
without permission. For information address:
The Berkley Publishing Group, 200 Madison Avenue,
New York, New York 10016.

ISBN: 0-515-11478-2

A JOVE BOOK®
Jove Books are published by The Berkley Publishing Group,
200 Madison Avenue, New York, New York 10016.
JOVE and the "J" design are trademarks
belonging to Jove Publications, Inc.

PRINTED IN THE UNITED STATES OF AMERICA

10 9 8 7 6 5 4 3 2 1

ONE

Clint had just crossed from Oklahoma into Texas, with intentions of heading south, when he heard the shots.

"Whoa boy," he said to Duke, reining him in.

Clint sat his horse quietly, trying to locate the direction from which the shots were coming. Judging by the sound, there was a running gun battle going on. Clint finally decided on a direction and headed west. He wanted to see what was going on. If both sides of the battle were evenly matched, there'd be no need for him to interfere. He could continue on his way. If, however, somebody needed help, he was too nearby to ignore that fact.

Clint rode Duke at a gallop and as he topped a rise the shots became much clearer. Looking down he saw that three Conestoga wagons were under siege. They were being circled by mounted men who appeared to be a mixture of whites and Indians—more likely Comancheros, about a dozen of them. As he watched, he realized that most of the shots were being fired by the men on horseback. The shots coming back from the wagons were few and far between. In fact, they were so few that the only reason the Comancheros hadn't charged the wagons must have been because they were having too much fun. As soon as they started having less fun, they'd charge for sure.

The people in the wagons needed help.

Clint had two options open to him. He could charge the Comancheros, firing as he did so, but would they run from one man? Maybe not, no matter how accurately he might be firing.

His second option was to find a vantage point within range where he could fire from cover. That way they wouldn't know how many men were firing at them. Rather than find out, they might simply flee.

The second option was obviously the best.

He looked around and saw that if he circled the action there was a rise that was well within range. From here he'd have to make every shot perfect. He decided to try to get closer and hoped that the Comancheros wouldn't run out of fun before then.

He turned Duke and rode hard for the closer rise. As they approached, he pulled his rifle from the scabbard and dismounted even before the big gelding had come to a stop.

He threw himself onto the ground and sighted down the barrel of his rifle. He was plenty close enough, and his first shot took a man right from his saddle as if he'd been jerked by a rope. It had the desired effect on the other men as they stopped and looked around, trying to see where the shot had come from. Clint sighted and fired again, and another man fell. He fired rapidly after that, some shots just for effect. He killed two more before someone shouted and waved—possibly the leader—and they turned their horses and rode off.

Clint remained where he was until the fleeing men were out of sight, then stood, mounted Duke, and rode down to the wagons.

Before approaching the wagons, he dismounted and walked over to each of the fallen men to make sure they were dead. Three of them were white men and one was an Indian. Their horses were nearby, standing easily and munching on the ground. They had been around a lot of gunfire and were not the kind of animals who would run off, spooked. One of them, an Indian pony, was a particularly good-looking animal.

Clint turned and looked at the three wagons, which had been pulled up close to each other. Each one was pulled by a team of two horses, and one of them had both animals on the ground, riddled with bullets. Somehow, the other horses had escaped harm.

Holding Duke's reins, Clint started walking toward the wagons, wondering why no one had come out from cover yet.

"Hello the wagons!" he shouted.

"Don't come no closer," a voice called out. It was a male voice—or so he thought. Deeper than a woman's, but somewhat higher than a man's.

"Look, the danger is past," Clint said, "but you'll have to get moving before they get brave and come back."

"I said don't come no closer or I'll shoot," the voice said, shaking with nervousness, or fear.

"Who's in charge?" Clint asked.

"I am," the same voice said.

"Well then come out so we can talk."

There was a moment's hesitation and then the voice said, "Go away."

"Hey, I helped you out here," Clint said. "The least I deserve is a thank-you, don't you think?"

Clint heard a murmur of voices and frowned because it didn't sound like men and women talking. It sounded like—no, it couldn't be!

"Look, whoever's in charge come on out."

"I'll shoot."

"You didn't do so well when you had a dozen targets, how well are you going to do now that you have one?"

Again the buzz of odd sounding voices and then the voice said, "Okay, we're comin' out."

Clint waited. The first thing he saw was the long barrel of a rifle, and then the person holding the gun came into view. He was tall and gangly but couldn't have been more than sixteen.

And he looked plenty scared.

"You're in charge?" Clint asked.

"That's right."

"Well . . . where are your parents?"

"Ain't got none."

"Well, what about adults?"

"There ain't any."

Clint was stunned.

"No adults?"

The boy held the rifle tightly and shook his head, then turned and said, "Come on out."

They came out one by one, boys and girls, dirty, sweaty, scared, and none older than the sixteen-year-old holding the rifle. There was one other gun, a rifle in the hands of a black-haired girl who looked about thirteen. All of the other children—nearly twenty of them—looked to be twelve or under.

"What the hell are a bunch of kids doing out here all alone?" Clint asked.

TWO

Before he could ask the question again, the girl with the rifle said, "Mister, Andrea's hurt and we don't know what to do for her."

"Did she get shot?"

"Yes."

"Let me have a look, then—" he said, and started forward, but the boy with the rifle aimed it at him, stopping him in his tracks.

"Don't come no closer."

"Eddie," the girl said, "he's got to help Andrea."

"Put the gun down, Eddie," Clint said. "The bad guys are gone, and I'm the good guy, but they're not going to stay gone for long."

"Eddie, listen to him!" the girl said.

"What do you say, Eddie?"

The boy thought a minute, biting his lip, and then lowered the rifle.

"Okay."

"You want to get out of here alive?" Clint asked them all.

"Yes," Eddie said.

"You take me to see Andrea," Clint said to the thirteen-year-old girl. "Eddie, you and the others get those two dead horses unhitched and back the wagon away from them. You're going to need a new team."

"Where we gonna get one?" Eddie asked.

"There are four Comanchero horses out there," Clint said. "Think you can catch them?"

Eddie puffed out his chest and said, "Sure I can."

"Good, then get two—oh, and the Indian pony. Make sure you catch three of them, including the pony. Understand?"

"We understand," a girl of about eight said. She had blond hair worn in pigtails.

"Well good," Clint said to her, "then get to it." He looked at the black-haired girl and said, "What's your name?"

"Nancy."

"Take me to Andrea, Nancy."

"This way."

She grabbed his hand and started dragging him to one of the wagons. The other kids were scattering to do what he'd told them to do. The question of what they were doing there was going to have to wait—but his curiosity wouldn't allow it to wait too long.

Nancy took him to one of the wagons. He thought the injured girl would be inside, but instead she was on the other side of it, up against one of the rear wheels. She was wrapped in a blanket, her head and blond hair soaked with sweat. She appeared to be about the same age as Eddie, maybe a year older.

"Hello, Andrea," he said, crouching down by her.

"W-who are you?" Her eyes were wide with fright, and maybe shock.

"He's gonna help you, Andy," Nancy said.

"My name's Clint, Andrea," he said. "Where are you shot?"

"My s-side, I think," she said.

"Does it hurt?"

"I-it's kinda numb..."

"All right, let me have a look."

She allowed him to open the blanket. Beneath it she was wearing a boy's shirt and trousers. The left side of the shirt was soaked with blood.

"Nancy, do you have any water?"

"Sure."

"And I'll need something to use for bandages."

"Right."

Nancy got up and ran to get what he asked for.

Clint tore the shirt open, peeling the fabric away from the bloodstained area. He touched her gently, trying not to hurt her, but he had to find the wound. When he did, he found that the bullet had gone right through the flesh on her side without hitting anything vital. In fact, the bleeding had almost stopped by itself.

The girl gritted her teeth and remained very still while he examined her.

"Am I g-gonna die, mister?" she asked.

"No, honey," he said, "you're going to be just fine. Just stay still."

"You ain't lyin' to me?"

"No, I'm not lying."

Nancy returned with a basin of water and some cloth for bandages. Clint washed the wound, examined it more closely, and saw that his earlier finding was correct. It was a through hole, and not a particularly bad one. He tore the cloth and made a bandage, then wrapped it around her waist nice and tight.

"Does that hurt?" he asked.

She bit her lips and said, "No."

He smiled.

"You're a brave girl." He turned to Nancy and asked, "Did anyone else get hurt?"

"No, mister."

"Nancy, why don't you stay with Andrea, give her something to drink, and I'll be right back. Okay?"

"Okay, mister."

"I'll be right back," he said to the injured girl.

"Thanks, mister."

"Sure."

He left the two girls and went to find the boy, Eddie. It was time to get some answers.

THREE

"I thought I saw just one man," Clark Day said.

"How could one man shoot like that?" Matt Carpenter demanded.

"How many men did you see?" Ray Jennings asked Carpenter.

"I didn't see nobody," Carpenter said.

"What about the rest of you?" Jennings asked of the remaining Comancheros. Jennings had been the leader of this bunch for over three months now, since he'd killed the previous leader in a knife fight.

The other five exchanged glances with each other and all shook their heads. They hadn't seen a thing.

"We was concentratin' on the wagons," one of them, a man named Byers, said.

"We shoulda took them wagons right off," Carpenter said.

Jennings turned on Carpenter and said, "Are you callin' the shots now?"

Carpenter tried to match Jenning's glare but eventually averted his eyes.

"No, I ain't, but—"

"Then shut the hell up," Jennings said.

They were camped several miles away from the place where they had attacked the three wagons. The Conestogas had looked like such easy pickings that they had decided to have some fun before taking them. Maybe that was a mistake, but Ray Jennings was damned if he'd admit that much in front of his men.

Once they'd realized that no one was chasing them, they had camped and were now discussing the situation.

"What are we gonna do, Ray?" Byers asked.

"We're gonna get those wagons, that's what we're gonna do," Jennings said. "There couldn'ta been more than two guns against us."

"Yeah, and how many that we couldn't see?" Carpenter asked.

"One," Clark Day insisted. "I only saw one rider."

"Why didn't you say something back there?" Jennings asked.

"I couldn't get your attention," Day said.

"Shit."

"Couldn'ta been one gun, Ray," Carpenter said. "Not shootin' like that."

"Well," Jennings said, "we're gonna go back and find out, ain't we?"

"Just the eight of us?" Byers asked. "What if Carpenter's right, what if there is more than one? What if there's . . . a dozen or more."

Jennings looked at Clark Day.

"When are we supposed to meet up with Con and the others?"

Day looked up at the sun, then said, "I figure a

few hours from now. Con's usually on time."

Con Able was Ray Jennings's competition for leadership of the Comancheros. Able had backed Jennings's play against the former leader, but now Jennings was sure that Able wanted to take the leadership from him.

"How many men's he got with him?" Jennings asked.

"Same as we had," Day said, "twelve."

"All right, then," Jennings said, "we'll meet up with Con and then we'll go after them wagons."

"You think them wagons are worth it, Ray?" Byers asked.

"I don't know, Jim," Jennings said. "I guess that's somethin' else we're gonna find out, huh?"

"If you say so," Byers said.

Jennings looked around and said, "Shit, we lost Cunning Dog."

Cunning Dog was an Apache who had been their best tracker, but none of them had trusted him, and they knew he hated them.

"So what?" Carpenter asked. "That redskin woulda cut all our throats some night if he ever thought he could get away with it."

"We'll need a tracker," Jennings said.

"We can track—" Carpenter started to say.

"We need a good tracker," Jennings said, cutting him off.

"Con's got Painted Man with him."

"There's another one—" Carpenter said.

"Shut up, Carpenter!" Jennings said. "That's good," he said to Day. "Painted Man's a damn good tracker. We'll meet up with them and then we'll go and get our wagons."

FOUR

When Clint found Eddie, the boy was holding the reins of the Indian pony in his right hand, looking extremely proud of himself. He held his rifle in his left hand. Some of the other children were holding the reins of two more horses. The wagon had been unhitched from the dead team and backed away from them.

"Good job, Eddie," Clint said.

"Thanks. How's Andy?"

"She's going to be fine," Clint said, "just fine."

"That's good."

"Is she older than you?"

"Yeah," the boy admitted, "but I'm the oldest boy."

"I see. Look, Eddie, I've got a lot of questions, but first I think we ought to get these horses hitched up to the wagon and then we can get going."

"To where?"

"Where were you headed?"

"California."

"Where were you coming from?"

"Missouri?"

"So you came through Oklahoma?"

"Yes, sir," Eddie said. "Isn't that how we get to California?"

"Well, it's one way," Clint said. Actually, if he was heading from Missouri to California he wouldn't be this far south. He would have just gone through Kansas and into Colorado. He could deal with that later.

"I don't think we'll head that way just yet, though," Clint said. "I just want to get you and the others away from here, in case those men come back."

"You scared them off once," Eddie said, "even killed some of them. Couldn't you do it again?"

"Well, when they come back this time they might have help," Clint said. "I think we'd better get going. Come on, help me hitch these horses up."

Clint tied the Indian pony to one of the other wagons and then he, Eddie, and some of the other children hitched up the two new horses to the first wagon.

"Now we'll get Andrea into one of the wagons and get going."

"Who's gonna drive the wagons?" Eddie asked.

"Who was driving them before?"

"Me one, Andy another, and Nancy the last one."

"Well, we'll let Nancy drive the wagon with Andrea in it, and you can drive another. Can any of the other kids drive?"

"Sam," Eddie said. "He's twelve."

"All right, then Sam will handle the other one."

Clint would have driven it himself, but he wanted to be astride Duke if anything happened.

"I tied the pony to the back of the last wagon."

"Why are we takin' it?" Eddie asked.

"Well . . . maybe at some point you'll want to ride it."

"Okay!" Eddie said enthusiastically.

"And maybe you can explain to me what all you kids are doing out here."

"Sure," Eddie said, "I guess. We really don't have folks—"

"Wait, wait," Clint said. "Let's get everything done and get under way first. Come on."

Once they had the new horses hitched to the wagon, and Andrea inside one of the wagons, the other children climbed aboard. Eddie drove the lead wagon, then Sam the second, and Nancy the last. Since Sam was less experienced than the others, Clint wanted his wagon in the middle.

Watching the children pile into the wagons, Clint realized that there was an equal amount of boys and girls, ten each. The youngest seemed to be four or five, and there seemed to be about two each in most of the age brackets, on up through sixteen and seventeen. Eddie was sixteen and Andrea—as he had now found out—was seventeen, which put them roughly in the same age bracket.

"Where are we headin'?" Eddie asked.

Clint thought it best for them to get out of Texas altogether. That meant going back to Oklahoma, or north to Kansas. If their ultimate destination was California, it seemed to make more sense to go into Kansas. They'd still have to go through a small part of Oklahoma, but at least they wouldn't be retracing their steps.

"Kansas, through Oklahoma," Clint said.

"Back into Oklahoma?"

"We'll go north, right through Oklahoma into Kansas. We'll find someplace there to stop and maybe have a doctor look at Andrea. After that we can talk about what's going to happen—and about what's already happened. Okay?"

"Whatever you say, mister," Eddie said.

"Clint, Eddie," he said, "my name is Clint."

"Okay, Clint."

They headed north, Clint's curiosity still eating him up, but this wasn't the time to get the full explanation.

Soon, though . . . real soon.

FIVE

They traveled until nightfall, and when they camped in Oklahoma, Clint hoped they had put enough distance between themselves and the Comancheros. If they came back, he would no longer have the element of surprise on his side. As good as he was with a gun, eight-to-one odds were long.

Clint told Eddie to have someone take care of the horses and start a fire.

"Who does the cooking?" he asked.

"Andrea."

"Well, that's out," Clint said. "She won't be cooking tonight. Who else?"

"Maybe Nancy."

"What about you?"

"Me?" Eddie looked at him as if he were crazy. "I'm a man. Men don't cook."

"Who told you that?"

Eddie stared at him.

"I . . . don't know, I just—"

"Never mind," Clint said. "Just get the fire started. Either Nancy will cook or I will."

"You?"

"Just do it, Eddie."

Clint left Eddie and the others to carry out their chores and went to check on Andrea.

"You're crazy, Andy," Nancy said.

"I'm serious, Nancy," Andrea said. "When he touches me, I feel like a woman."

"You're wounded, for heaven's sake."

"I'm still a woman," Andrea argued. Nancy was the closest girl to her age, and the two often confided in each other.

"I think he likes me," Andrea said.

"Andy," Nancy said, "he's a grown-up."

"What do you think I am?" Andrea's tone was indignant. "I'm seventeen, Nancy. Most girls my age are married already."

"You want to marry him?" Nancy asked, in shock. "You just met him. Besides . . . he's so old!"

"He's not that old."

"What makes you think he likes you?" Nancy asked. "You hardly talked."

"It's the way he touches me," Andrea said, a dreamy look in her eyes. "He's so . . . so gentle."

"Andy, I think you—"

"Shh," Andrea said, "I think he's coming."

"I don't hear any—" Nancy started to say, but the flap of the wagon was thrown aside and Clint Adams climbed inside with them.

As Clint entered the wagon, he had the feeling he'd interrupted something.

"How is she, Nancy?"

"She's okay, Mr. Adams."

"Nancy, I told you to call me Clint."

"All right, Clint."

"Eddie tells me you can cook."

"Yes, I can," Nancy said. "Andrea usually does the cooking, though. She's really good. I'm just . . . passable, really."

"Well, Andrea's not going to be cooking tonight, so do you think you can?"

"Sure . . . Clint."

"Thanks."

Nancy started to climb out of the wagon, then she and Andrea shared a look that made Clint certain that he had interrupted them.

When Nancy was gone, Clint turned to Andrea.

"How are you feeling, Andrea?"

"I'm fine, really," she said. "It hardly hurts."

"Well, let me take a look at it."

Clint was afraid the wound might become infected, but when he lifted her shirt and undid the bandage, he saw that the wound was clean. He noticed then that Andrea was holding her shirt up for him, but higher than necessary. He could see the lower portions of her full breasts and just the hint of brown nipple. He caught himself staring longer than he should, however, and gently tugged her shirt down. He didn't know if she'd done it accidentally or on purpose, but he knew he shouldn't have been looking at the breasts of a girl so young—no matter how pretty they were.

"It's nice and clean, Andrea," he said. "It will heal nicely."

"You saved my life, Clint."

"I don't think you were ever in danger of dying, honey," he said.

Her cheeks colored as he called her "honey," and he vowed not to do it again. He now suspected he knew what the two girls had been talking about, and what he didn't need was a lovesick seventeen-year-old on his hands.

"I have to go and make sure everything is... going all right, Andrea, so I'll be back to check on you later."

"You're gonna leave me alone?"

He smiled and said, "I'll send some of the other children to stay with you. Nancy will bring you some food when it's ready."

"But I didn't mean—" she started, but he hurried out of the wagon, thinking that it was the best course of action to take.

SIX

"So, tell me a story," Clint said to Eddie.

Nancy had done no worse with bacon and beans than he could have done himself. However, he had made the coffee himself, since he was the only one who was going to drink it. All of the stores were his, for the children had very little of their own left.

All of the children were eating, and Clint had sent Nancy off with a plate for Andrea. That left him and Eddie sitting by the fire, and now he wanted his curiosity satisfied.

"What kind of story?" Eddie asked.

The boy seemed like a nice enough kid, but he didn't appear to be too bright.

"How did the lot of you get out here all by yourselves?"

"Well, we didn't get all the way out here by ourselves."

Clint waited, and when no more was forthcoming, he said, "Keep talking."

"Well, Dave and Phil, they came to Missouri to get us," Eddie said.

"Dave and Phil who?"

Eddie frowned.

"I think Andrea knows what their last names were."

"Okay, go on. Where were Dave and Phil from?" Clint asked.

"Well, California, naturally," Eddie said. "That's why we're headed there."

"Why are you headed there?" Clint asked.

"That's where Dave and Phil were taking us."

Clint closed his eyes, then opened them and tried again.

"Why were Dave and Phil taking you all there, Eddie?" he asked.

"So we could have new homes, with mothers and fathers," Eddie said patiently, as if Clint should know all of this already.

"What about your real parents?"

"We don't have any."

"None of you have real parents?"

Eddie nodded.

"Are you trying to tell me that you're all orphans?" Clint asked.

"Yes."

"And that these fellas Dave and Phil came all the way from California to take you back there to be adopted?"

"That's right."

"Why?" Clint asked. "I mean, why would they go all that way for children?"

"All I know is, the town they come from didn't

have no children," Eddie said. "That's what they told us."

"What happened to them?"

"They all died."

"How?"

"I don't know," Eddie said. "I think Andrea knows, though."

Clint saw that in order to fill in the gaps in Eddie's story he was going to have to talk to Andrea. He just hoped he was wrong about her having a crush on him—or worse.

"Eddie," Clint asked, "what happened to Dave and Phil?"

Eddie looked down and said, "They got killed."

"How?"

"We don't know for sure," the boy said. "They went into town to get some supplies, and they didn't come back. Me and Andrea went in looking for them after a few days and we found out that they got killed."

"By who?"

"We don't know."

"Did you talk to anyone?"

"Nobody would talk to us," he said. "They said we were just kids."

"Where did this happen?"

"Just after we got to Oklahoma."

"Do you remember the name of the town?"

Eddie thought a moment and then shook his head. "No."

Something else Clint was going to have to get from Andrea. He wondered why he was even trying to talk to Eddie.

"You've been in charge since then, Eddie?"

"Uh . . . well, yeah."

"What does that mean?"

"Well, Andrea was really in charge because she's, uh, smart and I'm not, but when she got shot, I took over. Besides, I'm the only one who can really shoot."

Clint didn't remember him hitting any of the Comancheros, but he didn't comment on that.

"Course, I never shot at people before," Eddie said. "I don't think I hit any of them."

"That's okay, Eddie."

The boy looked down and said, "My hands were shaking."

"That's okay, Eddie," Clint said again, "so were mine."

Eddie looked up quickly and said, "Really?"

"Yes, really," Clint lied.

Eddie's face brightened, and he reached for more beans. Clint decided not to ask him any more questions about the ordeal. He'd satisfy the rest of his curiosity by talking to Andrea.

SEVEN

Clint left Eddie sitting by the fire finishing his dinner and went to talk to Andrea. When he was finished with that, he'd set up watches with himself and Eddie. The rest of the children were too young.

"Andrea," he called as he reached her wagon. He didn't want to surprise Nancy and Andrea again as he had done before.

"Come on in, Clint," Nancy called.

Clint tossed back the flap and climbed into the back. Not only were Andrea and Nancy there, but several of the younger girls, as well. Apparently they were going to sleep in the wagon with Andrea.

"Can we talk, Andrea?" Clint asked.

He saw a look pass between Andrea and Nancy, and then the injured girl said, "Sure, Clint. Nancy, just take the kids outside for a few minutes, okay?"

"Sure, Andy."

After Nancy had left with the younger girls, Clint asked, "Andy? Is that what I should be calling you?"

"Oh no, Clint," Andrea said, "I like when you call me Andrea."

"All right, then," he said, sitting next to her. "How do you feel?"

"Fine," she said, then squirmed and added, "but it itches."

"That means it's healing. That's good."

"What did you want to talk to me about, Clint?"

"I was talking to Eddie about what brought all of you out here, but he didn't seem to know—or remember—a lot of facts."

"Eddie's not as smart as some of the others."

"Like who?"

"Oh, Nancy, and Sam, and even some of the smaller children. He's a good friend, though."

"I'm sure he is," Clint said. "Could you fill me in on some of the facts that he missed?"

"I can tell you the whole story, if you like," Andrea said.

"That would be great."

"Why do you want to know it, though?"

"I have to know what to do with all of you, Andrea," he said. "I can't just go off and leave you on your own."

"We have to go to California, Clint," she said forcefully. "That's where we have to go! There are people there who are waiting for kids, and these kids need fathers and mothers."

"What about you?"

"I'm too old to worry about that," she said.

"Then why did you come along?"

"To make sure the others got there," she said. "They need parents to take care of them. Eddie and me, we can take care of ourselves."

"So what's going to happen once you get the others to California?"

"Me and Eddie, we'll leave. Like I said, we can take care of ourselves."

"Can you?"

"Yes," she said, and then looked down at her wound. "Oh, this? This was just something new, something we hadn't run into before. Isn't that how you learn, Clint? By experiencing?"

"Yes, it is, Andrea."

"Then see? Now I've dealt with this—with your help, of course—and now I'll know for the future."

"I assume there are adults waiting in California to adopt these children."

"Yes."

"What if one of them wants to adopt you, or Eddie?" he asked.

"That ain't gonna happen!" she said. When she became agitated, her grammar worsened.

"Why not?"

"It didn't happen in Missouri, and it ain't gonna happen in California—and if we start looking forward to that, we're just gonna get disappointed . . ."

The word "again" was unspoken at the end of that sentence.

"Do you want to hear the story?" she asked.

"Yes, I do," he said. "Go ahead."

EIGHT

She made it brief, and told it with very little emotion in her voice. A tale of a small town in California that had no children because a disease had wiped them out completely. Although women were starting to have babies, it was only a few, and the town felt that without the presence of children, they would die. Not only were they missing the joy that children could bring to them, but they were missing the young adults who would later help the town to grow into a city. In short, they needed children to insure their future growth.

The town council got together and decided that they should go out and find children and bring them back. The only way they could think to do this was to find orphan children, children with no homes and families, and bring them back.

Entrusted with this mission were two men, Philip Carlton and David Gillette. These were the two men who came east looking for children and found them in Missouri—largely from the Springdale, Missouri, orphanage, which was overloaded with children. They had too many, they said, to adopt all of them out. In fact, some of them were too old to adopt—like Eddie and Andrea and, some thought, like Nancy and Sam. Potential parents, the orphanage headmistress said, wanted cute children, seven, eight, perhaps nine, but not much older.

Phil and Dave took the older children off the orphanage's hands. Others they gathered from the streets as they went along, until they had twenty-one children to take back to California with them.

At this point, Clint had questions....

"Wasn't it illegal for the orphanage to give up the older children like that?"

"Sure, it was," Andrea said, "but Mrs. Riley—she was the headmistress—she didn't care—and neither did we. We wanted to get out of that place, legally or not. Can you blame us?"

No, he couldn't.

"How many of you are from that orphanage?"

"There's me, Eddie, Nancy, Sam, Joey and Cissy—they're eleven—Johnny and Rachel—they're ten—and Denise. She's nine. Oh, and then there's Darlene. She's eight."

"Eight? What is she doing here?"

Andrea looked away.

"You stole her?"

"She wanted to come," Andrea said. "She was friends with Cissy, and Rachel and Nancy, and me. She wanted to come, so we took her."

"Which one is she?"

"She has blond hair in pigtails."

Clint remembered her from when he first arrived.

"Do you think the orphanage will be looking for her?" Clint asked.

"I don't think so."

"Why not?"

"Because we could tell what Mrs. Riley did. Like you said, it wasn't legal. She could get into a whole lot of trouble."

"You've thought this out."

"Yeah, we have—and we don't want her to get in trouble. She did what she thought was right for the orphanage, and for us."

Clint wondered if that was true. Was the woman trying to help the older children or just get rid of them?

"So ten of you are from the orphanage?"

"Right."

"And the other eleven?"

"There's ten more," she said. "Willy got killed along the way."

"How?"

"He got bit by a snake. Wasn't nothin' Phil or Dave could do for him. He just blowed up and died."

Clint knew she meant the boy had swelled up. In addition to the snake venom being deadly, he must have been allergic to it.

"Okay then, the other ten are from the streets?"

"Yes."

"All of them?"

She hesitated.

"Andrea, if I'm going to help you, I have to know everything."

"Two of the children were bought by Phil and Dave," she said.

"Bought?"

She nodded.

"From who?"

"From their folks."

"You mean to tell me that two of these children were sold by their mother and father?"

"Yes."

"Jesus . . . how could parents sell their own kids?"

"They was poor, and they needed money."

"Are both kids from the same family?"

"Yes," she said. "Their folks had nine kids and couldn't feed them all."

"So they sold two of them," Clint said, shaking his head in wonder. "How did they pick the two?"

"I don't know."

"Did they pick them, or did Phil and Dave?"

"The folks did. They just asked Phil and Dave if they wanted two, and when they said yes, they gave them Garth and Wynona."

"Just like that?"

"Just like that . . . for money."

"How much?" Clint asked.

He wondered what the going rate was for two children being sold by their own parents.

"I don't know," Andrea said. "Phil and Dave never told us."

"Andrea, what's the name of this town you were heading for, and where in California is it?"

"The town is called Ceremony," she said. "I don't know where it is."

"How did you plan on finding it, then?"

She shrugged.

"I figured to get us to California, and then start askin'," she said.

It was as sound a plan as any, he guessed.

"All right, then," Clint said, "suppose you tell me what happened to Phil and Dave."

NINE

"Near as I can figure," Andrea said, "they tried to steal a child in Castle Rock, Oklahoma."

"What?"

"That's what they were accused of," she said. "Didn't Eddie tell you?"

"Eddie said he didn't know what happened," Clint said. "He said you did."

"Well, Eddie doesn't want to know what happened. I think Eddie was getting too close with Phil. He thought Phil was going to adopt him. After Phil was killed—well, Eddie didn't take it too well."

"How were they killed?"

"I can only tell you what we heard when we went to town," she said. "We heard that they were shot for trying to steal a child."

Clint was starting to realize that Andrea was not only smart, but she was wise beyond her years.

"What do you think happened, Andrea?"

"I think they saw an opportunity to get another child. Somehow, they were misunderstood. Someone started shooting, and that was that."

"They wouldn't have actually tried to steal a child, would they?"

"No," she said, with a wry smile that belied her youth, "I'm the only one who stole a child."

"Maybe they tried to buy one?"

"Maybe," she said, with a weary sigh. "All I know is we went to town to find them and they were dead. After that we were on our own."

"How long ago was that?"

"I don't know," she said, with a shrug. "About a month, I guess."

"And you've managed to keep these children going all that time?"

"Eddie and I have."

"I think Eddie is probably only doing what you tell him to do."

"Eddie's been real helpful," she said defensively. "He's the one who's been going into towns to get supplies for us."

"With what?" Clint asked. "Do you have any money?"

"We only had what Phil and Dave left with us when they went into town," she said. "I've been spending that as little as possible."

"And then what?" he asked. "Where have you been getting your food?"

"Eddie's been hunting for us," she said. "He's really a very good shot. He just got flustered when he had to shoot at men who were shooting at us."

"I can understand that," Clint said. "In fact, he and I had a talk about it."

"Really?" she asked. "That's wonderful. I was worried that he'd never forgive himself."

"I think he'll be okay now."

"We'll all be okay now," she said. "We have you to get us to California."

"Me?" Clint said. "Wait a minute—"

"You saved our lives, Clint," she said, grabbing his hand and holding it tightly. "You're responsible for us now."

"Andrea—"

"We have to get to Ceremony."

"You still want to go on?"

"We have to go on," she said. "It's the only chance these children have for a home."

She said "these children" like a woman who was a dozen years removed from her own childhood, not a seventeen-year-old girl.

"What about Missouri?"

"We can't go back," she said. "I won't go back to that orphanage, and neither will Eddie or the others. They would have to go back to the streets. California has to be better for them than that, doesn't it?"

He couldn't argue with her there.

"Yes," he said, "it does."

"Then you'll help us?" she asked. "You'll take us to Ceremony?"

"Andrea," he said, "why didn't Phil and Dave just take you all by train? It would have made the trip much easier for everybody."

"They couldn't afford it."

That made sense. Who could afford to buy train tickets for twenty-one children?

"Clint, please," she said, holding his hand more tightly, "you have to help us. There isn't anyone else."

Clint thought fast but couldn't seem to come up with a reply that would keep him off the hook, and not upset Andrea.

"All right, Andrea," he said, "I'll help you get to California."

"Oh, that's wonderful!" she said, clapping her hands like a child—the child she should be, he thought. Circumstances had forced her to grow up much faster than she should have.

"I can't promise that I'll take you there myself, you understand," he said. "I'll just try to make sure you get there safely."

"I'll settle for that,." she said, "for now."

TEN

As Clint left Andrea's wagon, Nancy and the other girls—including Darlene, the stolen girl—climbed back inside, each bidding Clint a good night.

"Good night, girls."

He walked back to the fire, where Eddie was sitting, talking to Sam.

"Sam, how good are your eyes and ears?" Clint asked.

"They're really good, sir."

"You don't have to call me sir, Sam," Clint said. "You're not in the orphanage now."

"Yes, sir."

"Eddie, the three of us are going to stand watch," Clint said to the older boy. "Is Sam up to it?"

Sam turned pleading eyes toward Eddie, who wilted beneath them.

"He can do it, Clint."

"Yeah!"

"All right," Clint said. "Sam, are you sleepy?"

"Not a bit . . . sir."

"All right, then," Clint said, "you'll stand the first watch, and you'll wake me in three hours. Do you have a watch?"

"Oh, no, I don't—"

"Use mine," Eddie said. He took out a beautiful gold watch on a chain and handed it to Sam.

"That's a beautiful watch, Eddie," Clint said.

"Thanks."

"Where'd you get it?"

"I don't know," he said. "They told me I had it when I showed up at the orphanage."

"How old were you then?"

"I don't know," he said, with a shrug. "About five, I guess."

"You were in that orphanage for eleven years?" Clint asked in surprise.

"I guess," Eddie said. "See, nobody ever wanted to adopt me because I'm not smart."

"Oh, I don't think that's the reason, Eddie," Clint said.

"It is, really," Eddie said. "See, I'm kinda slow, and stupid. I gotta be told things twice."

"Eddie—"

"I mean it."

"Eddie, what about Andrea?"

The boy frowned.

"What about her?"

"She's smart," Clint pointed out, "and she was never adopted."

Eddie stared at Clint for a few seconds, then brightened and said, "Oh, yeah!"

"So you see?" Clint asked. "How smart you are or aren't had nothing to do with you not being adopted."

Eddie looked pleased for a moment, then frowned again.

"Then what was the reason?"

"Oh, something else," Clint said. He started groping at straws and decided to employ humor.

"Maybe it's just that you're ugly."

Eddie looked shocked, and Clint realized that the joke had gone completely over the boy's head.

"Eddie," he said hurriedly, "it's a joke, son, just a joke."

Eddie frowned for a moment, then brightened and said, "Oh, yeah," and started laughing.

"Sir?" Sam said.

"Sam," Clint said, "I told you, you don't have to call me sir."

"Then what do I call you?"

"Call me by my name, Clint."

Sam's eyes widened, as if the prospect of calling a grown-up by his first name was totally new to him—and it probably was. Even now he was struggling with it, so Clint decided to take him off the hook.

"What did you want to ask me, Sam?"

"Oh," Sam said. "Uh, what am I supposed to do when I'm on watch?"

"You watch with your eyes," Clint said, "and your ears."

"Huh?"

"You look and listen, Sam," Eddie said, "and if you see or hear anything suspicious, you wake us up."

Eddie wasn't as dumb as he thought he was—or as people had been telling him.

"Wake *me* up, Sam," Clint said, amending Eddie's statement. "Wake me up first. Do you understand what you have to do?"

"Sure," Sam said, "I watch and listen for three hours, then I wake you up, but if I see or hear anything suspicious, I wake you up right away."

"Right."

"Clint?"

"Yes."

"There's just one more thing."

"What's that, Sam?"

"What's something suspicious?"

ELEVEN

"I hear horses," Clark Day said.

"It's about damn time," Ray Jennings said.

He stood up and the others did, as well, some with their guns in hand, others simply ready to draw them if the need arose.

"Hey the fire!" a man's voice called out.

"That's Con. Put up your guns," he said to his men. Then he called out, "Come ahead, Con!"

Con Able rode into the light of the fire, followed by Painted Man and seven other men. One of the men had an arm in a sling, and another a bandage on his head.

"What the hell happened to you?" Jennings asked.

Able dismounted and faced Jennings.

"We lost three men. Darryl and Eric got shot up, but we got the money."

"Well," Jennings said, "that's better than we did. Sit by the fire and I'll fill you in."

While the other men took care of the horses, Jennings and Able sat by the fire and talked.

"So we got seventeen men," Able said. "That should be enough to handle your three wagons, but are you sure it's worth goin' after them?"

"I want them!" Jennings said tightly. "That's reason enough for me."

Able looked as if he wanted to argue the point, then decided against it. It wasn't time to make his move yet, he decided.

"All right, then," he said. "We better get rested up so we can get an early start. We don't know how far they got since this afternoon."

"It don't matter how far they got, or in what direction," Ray Jennings said. "We'll find 'em. Painted Man will track 'em, and I'll have those wagons, and the man who shot at us."

"You believe Clark?" Able asked. "That it was only one man?"

"He's the only one who saw anything," Jennings said, "so I'll take his word."

"One man," Able said, shaking his head. "Must have been some man."

"A dead man," Jennings said. "Whoever he is, he's a dead man."

TWELVE

Clint kept one eye open all during Sam's watch. He had to laugh to himself every so often as Sam lifted his head to listen or stood up to look when he thought he heard something. A couple of times Clint thought the boy was going to run over to him to wake him, but he resisted. He was surprised to find that he had dozed off, when Sam shook him awake.

"It's your turn to watch, sir," the boy said.

"Sam, I told you," he said, "call me Clint."

"Yes, sir," Sam said, "I will."

"Okay," Clint said, putting his hand on the boy's shoulder, "go and get some sleep."

"Can I ask you a question first... Clint?" Sam asked.

"Sure," Clint said, rolling out of his bedroll. "Just let me get a cup of coffee."

Clint went over to the fire and poured himself a cup. Since he was the only one drinking it, there was plenty left. He also saw that Sam had been studious about keeping the fire going.

"What's your question, Sam?" Clint asked.

The boy sat down next to him by the fire.

"Are we gonna die?"

Clint looked down at the boy, whose expression was very earnest.

"Well, I don't plan on dying, Sam," Clint said, "do you?"

"No, sir, but nobody ever plans on it, do they?" Sam asked. "It just happens, don't it?"

"Sometimes it does, yeah," Clint said. "But what makes you think it might happen here?"

"I don't know," Sam said, with a shrug.

"What are you thinking, Sam?"

"Nothin' has gone right since we left Missouri." The boy shrugged again.

"Well, that means that things should start going right now," Clint said.

"Whataya mean?"

"Things can only go wrong for so long, Sam," Clint said, "and then they have to start going right."

"Really?"

"Yes, really."

The twelve-year-old thought that over solemnly and then nodded and said, "That makes sense."

"Yes, it does," Clint agreed. "Now I think you should go and get some sleep. We're going to get an early start in the morning."

"Okay," Sam said, bounding to his feet. "Good night, Clint."

"Night, Sam."

He watched the boy run over to a wagon and crawl underneath, where he had a blanket. He swore the boy was asleep even before his head hit the ground.

Eddie had his bedroll near the fire, as Clint's was, and he asked, "Do you believe all that?"

"All what?" Clint asked, surprised that Eddie was awake.

"What you told Sam about things going wrong and right?" Eddie said.

"Sure I believe it."

"It would sure help if it was true," Eddie said sleepily. "We need some things to go right for a change around here."

Clint knew what he meant. These orphans needed some good luck for a change.

Was he the good luck?

THIRTEEN

Eddie had the last watch, and when Clint woke up, he saw that Nancy had joined him and started breakfast.

"How's Andrea?" Clint asked Nancy. "Did she sleep all right?"

"She slept fine," Nancy said. "We all did, for the first night in a long time."

He was slow this morning.

"Why is that?"

She looked at him and said brightly, "Because we have you now. Andrea says you're gonna get us to California. She says you're gonna take care of us."

"That's what she said, huh?"

"We don't have to worry anymore," Nancy said, and went back to making breakfast.

Clint walked over to Andrea's wagon and saw a little red-haired girl of about seven trying to get out.

"Here we go," he said, lifting her up and depositing her on the ground.

"Thank you," she said, and then added with a big smile, "and thank you for taking care of us."

Before he could say anything she turned and rushed off to join her friends, many of whom were now awake and making noise.

"Andrea," Clint called out.

"You can come in, Clint."

He climbed inside and found that she was there alone, making a face.

"I stink," she said. "I need a bath."

"Maybe later today," he said, "or I could bring some water in here for you."

"Would you? That would be nice."

"Sure," he said, "even though you've been playing dirty with me."

"Dirty?" she asked. "What do you mean?"

"I mean," he said, "you've been telling all the kids that I'm going to take care of them, and that I'm going to take them to California."

"I'm just trying to keep them from worrying any more," she said.

"By making promises to them that I can't keep?" he asked. "That's not the way to do it, Andrea."

She gave him a look that made him know that this one was going to be dangerous before she even got to be twenty years old. She was just naturally sexy, which was disconcerting at the moment, when she was only seventeen.

"Are you angry with me?"

"No, Andrea," he said, "I'm not angry. Just stop it, okay? Don't tell them any more without checking with me first."

"All right, Clint," she said, "I promise."

"I'll bring that water in for you and you can wash up," he said.

"Thanks. I'll feel so much better when I'm clean."

FOURTEEN

Clint had a couple of the bigger boys—other than Eddie and Sam there were a couple of eleven-year-olds who were able to do the job—bring some water to Andrea's wagon. Actually, it wasn't her wagon, it just happened to be the wagon she was recovering in. Clint could not afford to start thinking of her as being different from the other children. He had suddenly become responsible for twenty children, like it or not. That had happened when he took a hand while they were being attacked by a band of Comancheros, and yet there was nothing else he could have done. Accepting that, he also had to accept the consequences—the consequences being he was now charged with the safety of twenty children.

"Eddie," he said, "see that the rest of the teams are hitched up. I'll handle the first wagon."

"Right."

"What do you want me to do, Clint?" Sam asked.

"Make sure all the smaller kids are ready to move," Clint said.

"Right."

Clint handled hitching up the first team, and then saddled Duke for the trip—but a trip where? The only place he could think to take them was to the next town—whatever that was. There maybe he could hire someone to take them to Ceremony, California. Of course, he'd have to pay them with his own money. There was no way he could ever expect these children to pay that money back. Then, if he decided to take them to California himself, that would also cost money.

He wondered how much it would cost to put all of these kids on a train. He could always wire his bank for the money, if he was willing to invest that much money in the safety of kids.

Jesus, just by the way he put it to himself he had no other choice. And then there was Andrea. All of seventeen, how could she be so adept at manipulating a grown man already?

Face it, he told himself, how can you possibly win against twenty kids? If he left them on their own, he'd always wonder what happened to them, and he'd never forgive himself.

Once the teams were all hitched, Eddie came back to him and asked, "Where are we headed, Clint?"

"I don't know, Eddie," Clint said. "We'll just head north and see what town we come to."

"And then what?"

"We'll decide that when we get there."

Around midday Ray Jennings, Con Able, and the other Comancheros reached the point where they had attacked the three wagons and then been driven off.

"Painted Man," Able said, "take a look around."

Jennings watched as Painted Man went off to do as he was told. The Indian responded only to instructions from Con Able, and Jennings felt that Able would probably use this in the future as a tool to try to take over. Jennings made it a habit to watch the two men carefully whenever they were riding together.

"If there were only three wagons," Able asked, "why didn't you just ride up and take them?"

Jennings, annoyed at the question, said, "We needed the practice."

Able, knowing that he had annoyed Jennings, smirked and looked away. It wouldn't be long, he felt, before he was able to take over leadership from Ray Jennings. With incidents like this one, Jennings was doing part of the work for him, anyway.

Painted Man came back from his look around and spoke directly to Able.

"One man," he said. "That is all there was. He was there. . . ." He pointed up to the rise, the place where Clark Day said he saw only one man.

"I was right, then," Day said.

"Looks like it," Able said. He turned to Painted Man and said, "Can we track three wagons?"

"Yes."

"Is the man with them?"

"Yes."

"How do you know that?" Jennings asked.

Painted Man replied, looking at Able.

"He did not ride away alone."

"That don't mean he didn't separate from them later on," Jennings argued.

"That's true," Able said, "but we know that he left with them."

"He won't give us much trouble," Clark Day said. "Not with as many men as we have, and us knowing that he's all alone."

"Maybe not," Con Able said. "I guess we'll find that out when we catch up to them."

"Well, if we're gonna do that, we better get started," Ray Jennings said.

"Painted Man will ride on ahead," Able said. "If he locates them, he'll scout them and then come back and tell us."

"That's fine," Jennings said. "Let him go ahead."

Jennings would just as soon not ride with the Indian. Painted Man was the only man he was sure would back Con Able in a struggle for leadership. Without him around, Jennings knew that Able wouldn't try anything.

FIFTEEN

All the way to Kansas Clint was trying to figure out a way to get the children to California without taking them there himself. He finally decided that they'd stop in a town that had a telegraph office, and he'd start asking around for someone who wanted to help.

"Which town?" Eddie asked.

"A place called Alston," Clint said. "I think I might be able to find some help for us."

"To do what?" Andrea asked.

This was the first night since she'd been shot that she was sitting with them at the fire instead of eating in the wagon.

"Well, for one thing, we need to find someplace for all of you to stay until you head for California."

"Why don't we just go there?" young Sam asked.

"It's not that easy, Sam," Clint said.

"Why?"

Andrea leaned over and said, "I'll explain it to you later, Sam."

Sam nodded.

"Are you going to hire someone to take us to California?" Andrea asked.

"I'd prefer to come up with someone who would do it without pay."

"Why would they?" Eddie asked.

"Out of the goodness of their heart," Clint said, "or as a favor to me."

"You don't want to use your own money, do you?" Nancy asked.

"Nancy—" Clint started, but Andrea cut him off.

"Oh, Nancy, grow up," she said. "Why should he use his own money to send us to California? It's not even his responsibility to do anything for us. He's only helping because I—we asked him to."

Nancy looked away, embarrassed.

"If I had the money, Nancy, I would do it," he said. "In fact, there may come a time when I'll have to try and get enough money, but right now it's not time for that. Okay?"

"Sure, Clint," Nancy said, "I'm sorry."

"Nothing to be sorry about," Clint said. "If you have a question, you should ask it."

"I have a question," Eddie said. He even raised his hand, as if he were in school.

"What is it, Eddie?"

"Why would you do that?"

"Do what?"

"Use your own money?"

"I'd only do it if I wanted to, Eddie."

"And why would you want to?"

Clint looked around the fire. All of the children were there, and they were all waiting for an answer.

"Well, for one thing," he said finally, "I'd do it if

you stopped asking me so many questions."

Most of the children laughed, even the small ones, but they only laughed because the big ones did.

"No, seriously," Clint said, "I want to help you—all of you—and if using my own money is the only way I can do it, I will."

"We wouldn't want you to do that, Clint," Andrea said loudly, as if her tone of voice was supposed to tell the others to agree.

"Yes, we would."

Clint looked to see who had spoken and it was the little blond girl with pigtails, Darlene. She was the one Andrea had "stolen." All the children laughed again, and Clint joined in.

"Well, all right," he said, "some of you would."

After the children had gone to sleep, Clint divvied up the watches with Eddie and Sam again. Andrea wanted to take a watch, but he told her maybe in a few days. Actually, he hoped they'd be in town by then.

He allowed Sam the first watch again and actually slept a couple of hours. He was starting to think that maybe the Comancheros wouldn't even bother tracking them down. Maybe they'd figure it wasn't worth the effort.

He was sitting by the fire during his watch when he became aware that someone was coming toward him. As she got closer he saw that it was Andrea.

"You're supposed to be asleep," he said.

"I can't sleep," she said. "Can I sit with you for a while?"

"Sure you can."

She hunkered down by him and lowered herself to

the ground. She sat with her shoulder against the side of his leg. He was very conscious of the scent of her hair and the warmth of her shoulder. If he was a little younger—like ten or fifteen or twenty years—he'd be having different thoughts about her. It was bad enough she was so mature for her age, he just hoped she wasn't going to try to bring up some topic of conversation that would be uncomfortable.

"Clint?"

"Yes?"

"Have you made love to lots of women?"

SIXTEEN

"What?"

She looked up at him, the firelight casting flickering shadows on her pretty face.

"I know that's a personal question."

"It certainly is," he said. "What would make you ask a question like that?"

"I was just wondering."

"It's a little unusual for a young girl to be wondering something like that."

Instead of getting upset at being called a girl, she gave him a scolding look and said, "We both know I'm not a young girl, Clint."

"That may be so, but that's still not a proper question to be asking me."

"Well, maybe not," she said, "but I guess you just answered it for me, didn't you?"

"Andrea," he said warningly, "if you don't start talking about something else pretty quick, I'm going to boot your butt back to bed. Understand?"

"I understand."

They sat silently for a while, Andrea looking into the fire, Clint deliberately looking away from the fire so as not to destroy his night vision.

"Do you think those men will catch up to us?" she asked suddenly. "What did you call them?"

"Comancheros," he said.

"Yes, the Comancheros," she repeated, committing the name to memory now. "Do you think they'll come after us?"

"I wouldn't think so," he said. "Not once we left Texas, anyway. This would be a long way for them to track us, unless they knew it was worth their while."

"What would make it worth their while?" she asked.

"Money, women, some kind of goods they could sell," he answered.

"We don't have any of those things with us," she said. "Why would they have attacked us in the first place?"

"You were probably handy," he said. "They were passing by, they saw you and decided to see if you had anything of value."

"Couldn't they have done that without shooting at us?" she asked.

"That's their way," Clint explained. "Comancheros don't ask, Andrea, they just take."

"They sound like horrible men."

"They are."

"How do people get like that?"

"I can't answer that, Andrea," he said. "I'm not smart enough to tell you why people are the way they are."

"Are there a lot of people like that in the West?" she asked.

"I'm afraid there are."

"And are there a lot of people like you?"

"What do you mean, like me?"

"I mean good people," she said, "good men, like you."

Clint stared at the young woman and wondered what she would say when she found out about his reputation—and the longer he was around the children, the more likely it was that they would find out.

"There are all kinds of people everywhere in the world, Andrea," he said. "You can associate, or be friends with, whoever you want, and try to avoid the bad ones."

"Is that what you do?" she asked. "Try to avoid the bad ones?"

He hesitated, then said, "Yes."

"Then why did you help us?" she asked.

"Because I don't ignore people who are in need of help," he said.

"But there were so many of them and only one of you," she said. "You took a big chance for people you didn't even know."

"I had the element of surprise on my side, Andrea," he explained. "That counts for a lot."

"I can't believe how brave you were," she said. "You saved our lives—and then you saved me—"

Clint could see where this was leading and he decided to cut her off before she could go much further.

"Andrea, I think you'd better try to get some sleep. You still have some healing to do."

She stared at him for a moment, then said, "All right. Can you help me up?"

He put a hand beneath her arm and helped her to her feet. She was facing him then, very closely, and suddenly closed her eyes, as if she was expecting to be kissed.

"Good night, Andrea," he said.

She opened her eyes with a disappointed look on her face.

"Good night, Clint."

"See you in the morning for breakfast."

"I'm getting up early," she said, "to make breakfast myself."

"That's fine, as long as you feel up to it."

"I feel fine," she said, and then added, "thanks to you."

He watched her walk back to her wagon and wondered if he was going to be able to get out of this situation without hurting her feelings.

SEVENTEEN

Manly wasn't really a town in Kansas. It was a small group of shacks not far from the Oklahoma border that you would miss if you did not know it was there. Most outlaws knew of its existence, including Ray Jennings, Con Able, and the Comancheros.

As they crossed the border into Kansas, Jennings said, "We'll stop in Manly. Painted Man can go on ahead and look for some sign of the wagons."

"All right," Con Able agreed.

He didn't mind stopping in Manly. One of the things it did have was a whorehouse, as well as a saloon. It had been a while since Able was with a woman, and when that happened he often felt himself growing edgy.

When the Comancheros rode into Manly, they were recognized and eventually confronted by Tom Dewey. Dewey was the unofficial sheriff of this unofficial town. He and three deputies upheld the law—to a point. Visitors to Manly were allowed to do anything except rob it or burn it to the ground. That left a lot of leeway. All Dewey, his deputies, and the few residents of Manly wanted was for the place to still be there when outlaws—or, as in this case, Comancheros—left.

Dewey watched as the Comancheros rode in. He stood alone in the street, but anyone who had ever been to Manly knew that Dewey was never alone. He was always covered by one or two hidden deputies with rifles.

Jennings knew that he and his men were under at least two guns as he stopped in front of Tom Dewey. They had been there a few times before.

"Jennings, right?" Dewey asked. He was in his early thirties and had all the fame and fortune he could want right there in Manly. In every sense of the word he was the "Man" in Manly.

"That's right," Jennings said. "I remember the face, but—"

"Dewey," the sheriff said. Although he was called the sheriff, he wore no badge.

"That's right," Jennings said, "Tom Dewey, right?"

"That's right," Dewey said. "What are you and your boys here for, Jennings?"

"A little rest is all, Sheriff," Jennings said. "If that's all right with you, of course."

"That's fine," Dewey said. "How long do you intend to be here for?"

"One night, if that," Jennings said. "We might even pull out before nightfall."

"That's fine," Dewey said again. "You've been here before, you remember our rules?"

Jennings looked around and Able and the others nodded to him.

"We understand the rules, Dewey," Jennings said.

"Good," the unofficial lawman said. "Then I wish you and your men a good rest in Manly."

"Thanks, Sheriff."

Suddenly, Dewey turned his attention away from Jennings to Con Able.

"Hello, Con."

"Tom."

"You two know each other?" Jennings asked.

"We've seen each other a couple of times or so," Able said.

"Didn't know you were riding with anyone these days," Dewey said.

"For some months now, yeah."

"You usually ride alone."

"Thought I'd try this out."

"Painted Man around?"

Able nodded.

"He's around."

Dewey nodded, then stepped aside and allowed the Comancheros to pass.

"I'd like to put a bullet in that guy's head," Clark Day said.

"Why?" Able asked.

"Because badge or no badge he's still a no-good lawman."

"He's no more a lawman than you or me," Able said. "He's just trying to keep this place in one piece."

"I'd still like to plug him."

"You do that and you'd be dead before he hit the ground," Able said.

"Yeah, I know," Day said, "I heard about him and his deputies. I'd like to catch him without them just once, though."

"You'd never stand a chance against him."

"Why's that?" Day asked.

"He's just about the fastest man with a gun I've ever seen," Able said.

"Yeah, sure," Day said. But then he asked, "How fast?"

"Probably not as fast as, say, Clint Adams, but mighty close."

"Fast as the Gunsmith?" Day asked, his eyes wide.

"Pretty close."

Day reined his horse in enough to lag back and tell the others what he'd just learned.

"How well do you know him?" Jennings asked.

"I told you," Able said, "we've seen each other once or twice."

"Yeah," Jennings said, "enough times to be on a first-name basis, and for him to know that Painted Man rides with you."

"Right," Con Able said, "enough times for that."

And he didn't say any more.

EIGHTEEN

As the Comancheros were riding into Manly, Kansas, Clint was stopping the three wagons just outside of Alston, Kansas. They had come across a stand of trees that was large enough to mostly conceal all three wagons. There was still a possibility that the Comancheros would follow them, but Clint had to go into town to use the telegraph. He had no choice but to leave them alone, and this seemed a fairly safe place to do that.

"Why don't we just ride into town together?" Eddie asked.

"We'd attract too much attention, Eddie," Clint answered.

"From who?"

"From people whose attention we don't want to attract," Clint said.

"But I think it would be better if we stayed together," Eddie insisted.

"Believe me, Eddie," Clint said, "it's better this way."

Eddie walked off, and Clint frowned after him.

"Clint?"

He turned and saw Andrea standing next to him.

"What is it?"

"Eddie's afraid you'll do what Dave and Phil did," she said, "go away and not come back."

"I'll come back, Andrea."

"He's afraid you'll get killed, or something."

Clint thought a moment.

"Well, I suppose I could take him with me," Clint said, "but I'd rather leave him here to watch out for you and the rest of the children."

"Then tell him," she said. "He'll appreciate that, but you have to tell him that you'll be coming back."

"How did you get so smart so young?" he asked.

"I don't know," she answered truthfully.

Clint walked after Eddie and found him slumped against one of the wagons, his shoulders hunched.

"Hey, Eddie."

"Hi."

Clint put his hand on the boy's shoulder.

"I need your help, Eddie."

"To do what?"

"You understand that I have to go into town, don't you?"

"Yes," Eddie said grudgingly.

"Well, I need you to stay here and watch over the other kids."

"Why?"

"You're the oldest," Clint said, "and you know how to use the rifle."

"Sure," Eddie said, "I was a big help when they attacked the wagons."

"Actually, you were," Clint said. "You kept them

busy until help came. Hey, we talked about this before, fella. You did what you had to do."

"Yeah ... maybe ..."

"No maybe about it," Clint said. "I'm telling you the truth. Now, Eddie, you'll have to be real alert while I'm gone, understand?"

"I understand ... but ..."

"But what?"

Eddie turned and stared up at Clint.

"Y-you'll come back, won't you?"

"I'll be back, Eddie," Clint said, "don't worry."

"Y-you won't get killed?"

"I won't get killed, and I won't run off," Clint said. "I'll be back. Okay?"

Eddie nodded and said, "Okay."

"Good."

"Are you taking anybody with you?" Eddie asked.

"No," Clint said, "everyone is staying here. I shouldn't be gone that long, and this is a good place to camp. These trees will hide you from sight until I get back."

"W-what if those men find us?" Eddie asked. "O-or someone else."

"Just between you and me, Eddie, that's a possibility, but I have to go to town. I don't have a choice. I have to get some supplies, and I have to use the telegraph. Hopefully, I'll be back before anyone can come along and spot you. Can I depend on you to watch over everyone?"

"Sure you can, Clint," Eddie said. "You can count on me."

Clint took the boy by both shoulders and said, "I knew I could."

Eddie grinned.

"Why don't you go and get my gear together? I'll saddle Duke."

"I'll saddle him."

"He's kind of a temperamental cuss, Eddie. I don't want him to bite your hand off."

"He won't," Eddie said. "He already lets me pet him."

"He does?" Clint asked, frowning. "He doesn't usually let anyone but me touch him."

"Oh, he lets me," Eddie said enthusiastically. "We're buddies."

"Is that a fact?" Clint said. "Well, come on, then. This I've got to see."

NINETEEN

Con Able saw Tom Dewey come into the saloon and look around. He figured the man would come looking for him sooner or later. As it turned out, it was sooner.

Dewey went to the bar for a beer and carried it back to Able's table.

"Been a long time, Con," Dewey said, sitting across from him.

Able didn't say anything.

"What are you doin' with that bunch?" Dewey asked.

"What's wrong with them?"

"They're a bunch of losers, that's what's wrong with them," Dewey said. "You were a lot of things, as I remember, but you were never a loser."

"I'm still not."

"Then why them?"

"They're okay," Able said. "All they need is some direction."

"Right now they're getting that from Ray Jennings," Dewey said.

Able grinned.

"Not for long, huh?" Dewey asked.

"We'll see."

"Even when we rode together, Con, you were a loner. You won't last long with them, even as their leader."

Able took a sip of beer before answering.

"People change, Tom."

"Not you."

"But you have?" Able asked. "You're Sheriff of Manly, now?"

"Not a real sheriff," Dewey said, "but this place caters to some bad boys, Con. They needed somebody to take charge."

"You."

"Me as good as anybody else."

"And your men?"

"I've got some good boys working for me, Con," Dewey said. "I could use you, though."

"Me?"

"Sure, why not?" Dewey asked.

"I don't make a good deputy, Tom."

"Not as a deputy, then," Dewey said.

"As what?"

Dewey shrugged.

"Whatever you want to be. I could just use your gun to back me up."

"I thought you said you had some good boys."

"I do," Dewey said, "but none as good as you. You're about the best hand with a gun I ever saw, Con."

"Better than you?"

Dewey smiled.

"That's something we said we'd never find out, ain't it?" he asked.

"Well, if I stayed I think we'd end up finding out," Able said. "No, I think I'll keep riding with this bunch for a while, Tom."

"Suit yourself," Dewey said, "but keep the offer in mind."

"I will."

"Where are you headed when you leave here?" Dewey asked.

"Into Kansas," Able said.

"After what? A bank?"

"We don't do banks, Tom," Able said, "at least, not yet."

"Yeah, I know what Comancheros do, Con," Dewey said, "that's why I'm surprised to find you with them. You don't fit in with the type."

"Don't I?"

"You . . . had a problem when we rode together," Dewey said. "Uh, women . . . is that still a problem?"

Able started playing with his beer mug on the table, leaving wet rings on the surface.

"I would have thought you'd ask me that before you offered me a job."

"Is it?"

"No," Able said finally, "it's not a problem anymore."

Dewey studied his old partner for a few moments and then said, "Good," even though he felt the man was lying to him.

"That's good," Dewey repeated, standing up. "Well, I'd better be going."

"Going to keep an eye on us, Tom?"

"The others, yeah," Dewey said. "You just told me there's no reason to keep an eye on you . . . right?"

"That's right, Tom," Able said, nodding, "no reason at all."

Con Able watched Tom Dewey leave the saloon and wondered if he was going to have to kill the man before they left.

On the street outside, Tom Dewey was thinking the same thing about Con Able. They had ridden together successfully for a few years, but the problem that Able had with women soon drove them apart. Tom Dewey had no qualms about robbing a stage, or a bank, or even about killing someone who got in their way, but when it came to beating and raping women, he drew the line. He never knew what was inside of Con Able that forced him to do that to a woman, and he finally just gave up on trying to find out and they went their separate ways. That had been three years ago, and now Able was riding with a bunch of murdering Comancheros.

Con Able was right. People did change.

They got worse.

TWENTY

Clint rode into Alston and found it to be a small but bustling town, alive with activity and energy. He'd been past there before, but had never stopped. He'd never had a reason before.

Now he did.

The welfare of twenty children.

There'd been a time or two when Clint Adams had wondered what it would have been like to have children of his own. He'd long ago given up on that prospect, and yet here he was with the lives and welfare of twenty children in his hands.

Go figure.

On the way into town he decided that the best thing to do was send one telegram to his friend Rick Hartman in Labyrinth, Texas, and let Rick do the rest of the work for him. If anyone could find someone to take the kids off his hands, it was Rick. Hartman had more contacts throughout the West than anyone Clint knew, and he did it all from a small town in south Texas.

He found the telegraph office with no problem and left Duke just outside it. When he entered, he already had the telegram composed in his head, so he grabbed a pencil, wrote it out, and handed it to the telegraph clerk. The man read it over, moving his lips as he did so. Clint was able to read his lips as he went along:

RICK HARTMAN LABYRINTH TEXAS

NEED GUIDE TO TAKE 20 CHILDREN TO CALIFORNIA STOP PLEASE ADVISE SOMEONE RELIABLE FOR JOB STOP SMALL PAY LOTS OF SATISFACTION STOP NEED REPLY SOONEST STOP THANKS STOP

                              CLINT ADAMS
                              ALSTON KANSAS

"Twenty children?" the clerk asked.

"I had a lot of wives," Clint said. Then before the man could comment, he said, "Just send it."

"Yes, sir. Uh, where will you be when the reply comes in?"

"Probably the saloon."

"Which one?"

Clint made a face and said, "Check them both."

The clerk figured out the cost of the telegram—moving his lips as he did the math—and Clint paid him and left. He didn't know what to do with Duke. He wasn't going to be there long enough to put him up in the livery stable—he hoped. Even if Rick's reply didn't come right back, he wasn't going to be able to stay away from the children for long. After a couple of hours Eddie's newfound confidence would start to erode, and it would take more than Andrea had to keep it going.

He spotted one of the saloons across the street and decided to walk Duke over there and leave him outside while he got himself a beer.

He entered the saloon and found it doing a slight business at that time of the afternoon. The bartender was mopping the bar with a dirty rag and very little enthusiasm. When he saw that he had a customer, however, he perked up. He was a tall, slender man with pale skin and light blue eyes that were startling. He smiled broadly and lost a few years in Clint's estimation. He now figured the man for closer to thirty than forty.

"Hi, stranger," the man said, "welcome to the Alston Saloon. Whataya have?"

"Beer."

"Comin' up."

Clint leaned on the bar with his elbows and watched while the man drew the beer.

"You always this cheerful?" he asked as the man put the beer down in front of him.

"Naw," the man said, "just got up on the right side of the bed this morning—my wife's, if you know what I mean?"

"Is that unusual?"

"Are you married?"

"No."

"Ever been?"

"No."

"Then you don't know," the bartender said. "Anytime your wife lets you on her side of the bed you better take full advantage of it."

"Doesn't sound like a happy marriage."

"Aw, it's okay," the man said. "She's a good cook."

"That counts for a lot, does it?"

"An awful lot," the man said. "You wouldn't know it to look at me, but I like to eat."

He was right. When he touched his stomach, there was hardly any stomach there. Clint carried very little extra poundage, but this man made him look overweight.

"The name's Harris," the man said, putting out his hand, "Cosmo Harris."

"Cosmo?" Clint arched an eyebrow as he shook the hand.

"I know," the man said, making a face. "Folks around here just call me Harry."

"Glad to meet you, Harry," Clint said, releasing the man's hand. "My name is . . . Clint."

He decided right there and then to stick to his first name only.

"Glad to know ya, Clint. How long you gonna be stayin' in town?"

"Oh, just a couple of hours, probably."

"Got urgent business, huh?"

"Urgent enough."

"Yeah, lots of folks have urgent business these days. That's why I like bein' a bartender. All I got to worry about is pouring beer and whiskey."

"Sounds like the life, all right."

"Oh, it is, lemme tell you."

Sure, Clint thought, and then you go home to your wife at night.

He finished his beer and pushed the empty mug away from him.

"Want another?"

"No, one's enough," Clint said. Actually, another one wouldn't have been bad, but he wasn't in the mood for a talkative bartender. "Thanks."

"Sure."

As Clint was heading for the door, Harry called out, "Say, you come this way from the East?"

Clint turned.

"Why?"

"Thought you might've heard somethin' about that kid they're looking for."

Clint frowned.

"What kid?"

"Some family back East is missin' a kid. Thinks she's headed west with some other kids."

"Is that so?"

"Callin' it kidnappin'," Harry went on. "Might even be sendin' some law out this way to pick up their trail. See any kids out there?"

"No, Harry," Clint said, "no kids. See ya, okay?"

"Sure," Harry said, "stop in next time you're near here. You got one comin' on the house."

"Thanks," Clint said, and got out of there.

TWENTY-ONE

"Do you think he'll really help us?" Eddie asked Andrea.

"Of course he'll help us, Eddie," Andrea said. "All I have to do is ask him."

Eddie stared at her.

"You think he's in love with you, Andy?"

"No, I don't think he's in love with me," Andrea said, "but I know he wants me."

"How do you know?" Eddie asked.

"Men have wanted me since I was twelve, Eddie," Andrea said. "I think I can see it in a man's eyes by now."

"But . . ."

"But what?"

"But what if he's different?"

"How different could he be, Eddie?" she asked. "He's a man."

"I'm a man, Andy," Eddie said. "Well, almost, anyway. Am I different?"

She stared at him for a moment and then said, "No."

"What?"

"You want me, too, Eddie," she said. "I can see it in your eyes."

Eddie's eyes went wide. What Andrea said was true. He did want her, and she could see it. That meant she was telling the truth about men, and about Clint.

And what about him? he thought. He knew he was different. He loved her—although he hadn't told her as much. He'd tell her one day, though—when he got up the nerve.

"Andy?"

"Yes, Eddie?"

"W-what if he finds out what really happened to Phil and Dave?"

"He won't."

"And what about Darlene?"

"He won't find out about that either, Eddie. Stop worrying." Her tone was scolding.

"But . . . what if he does?"

"If he finds out anything we don't want him to find out, Eddie," Andrea said firmly, "I'll take care of him. Now stop worrying and let me cook. He's gonna expect food when he gets back."

Eddie took up his rifle and left Andrea by the fire.

As Eddie walked away, Andrea looked after him, shaking her head. Eddie was right, he was a man, and he was looking at her the way men had looked at her since she was twelve. That is, she noticed it when she was twelve. She didn't know what the look meant, actually, until the first time a man took her, when she was thirteen. She'd learned since then, though. She'd learned real well how to read the look and how to use it to her advantage.

In other words, by seventeen Andrea had learned to use men before they used her.

TWENTY-TWO

Con Able was spending most of his time in Manly in the saloon. He decided to stay away from the whorehouse, because despite what he had told Tom Dewey he still felt certain urges where women were concerned.

Even now there was a tightening in his groin and he could barely sit still. He was wondering if he should even keep fighting the urge when the batwing doors swung inward and Painted Man walked in.

The bartender noticed the Indian, opened his mouth as if to protest, and then thought better of it.

"Whiskey," Painted Man said, presenting himself at the bar.

"If you're sure you can handle it, chief," the bartender said.

"Whiskey," Painted Man said again, with a stolid expression.

"Comin' up."

The bartender poured a shot of whiskey for Painted Man and watched as the Indian poured it down. If the man expected smoke to erupt from Painted Man's ears, or something like that, he was to be disappointed. Painted Man put the empty glass down on the bar, turned, and walked to Con Able's table.

"Sit down," Able said. "You must be tired."

"I do not get tired."

Able waved a hand and said, "Yeah, I forgot."

Painted Man sat down, anyway.

"What have you got?"

"Kansas."

"Where?" Able asked. "In your pocket?"

Painted Man looked down at himself and said, "I do not have pockets."

"Jesus," Able said, "I forgot you got no sense of humor either."

Painted Man just sat and stared.

"All right," Able said, "what about Kansas?"

"That's where they went," Painted Man said, "Kansas."

"Where in Kansas?"

"I do not know."

"Well, where do you think?"

"Thinking," Painted Man said, "is what you do."

"Yeah," Able said, waving a hand again, "I forgot."

Suddenly, Painted Man sat forward and stared at Con Able.

"What?"

"You have it."

"Have what?"

"The look."

"What look?"

"The urge," Painted Man said, sitting back in his chair. "It has returned."

"No . . . it hasn't."

Painted Man shook his head.

"You can lie to me," he said, "but you cannot lie to yourself."

"Don't try any of your damned Apache wisdom on me," Able growled.

"You know it," Painted Man said, and fell silent.

Able was about to snap at the Indian when the doors swung inward again and Ray Jennings entered, followed by Clark Day and several others.

"I see your pet Indian is back," Jennings said, approaching the table. The others went up to the bar for whiskey.

Painted Man said nothing, just kept staring straight ahead.

"What did he find out?"

"The wagons went into Kansas."

"Then that's where we're goin'," Jennings said.

"Into Kansas? For three wagons? What was in those wagons, anyway?"

"I don't know, Con," Jennings said. "That's what we're gonna find out, isn't it?"

"I don't know, Ray," Able said, "chasing three wagons all the way into Kansas without knowing what's in them. We could be goin' a long way for nothin'."

"Not for nothin'," Jennings said, "never for nothin'. We'll get them back for that ambush."

"What ambush?" Able asked. "You ambushed them, remember?"

"Look," Jennings said, "if you don't want to go, you don't have to."

"Oh, I'm goin', all right," Able said, "don't worry about that."

"Then let's get movin'," Jennings said.

"Now?"

"Why wait?" Jennings asked.

"Painted Man just rode in," Able said. "He needs to rest."

"Let him rest, then," Jennings said. "We're pullin' out in an hour."

Jennings walked away, and Able stared at Painted Man, who said, "I do not get tired."

"Oh, shut up."

Painted Man just stared.

TWENTY-THREE

Clint intended to leave Alston immediately after leaving the saloon, without even thinking about the telegraph message he had sent. If what the bartender had said was true, Andrea had some explaining to do.

He had already mounted Duke and intended to ride him hard back to the camp where he'd left the children and the three wagons when an idea struck him. Instead, he rode Duke down the street, looking for the office of the town newspaper. When he found it, he dismounted and went inside.

He'd been in many newspaper offices, and there was always the oppressively noisy printing press going, and the smell of ink in the air. This one was no different. There were two people working inside, and both had ink-smudged faces and hands. Both were men, and neither were aware of his presence. The only way to alert them was to walk up to one and tap him on the shoulder. He did that, and the man just about hit the ceiling.

"Jesus!" he said, staring at Clint. "You scared me out of ten years' growth."

If that was the case, the man surely couldn't afford it. He was barely five six as it was.

"Sorry," Clint shouted. "Are you the editor?"

"I am."

"I need to talk to you."

The man made a face and grabbed a rag, wiping futilely at his hands.

"Come into the other room."

Clint didn't know there was another room. Newspapers were stacked so high that he hadn't noticed a second doorway. Now he followed the man into an office with a rolltop desk. The man closed the door, drowning out about half the noise of the printing press.

"I can't stop the press," the man said, "I'm on deadline."

"That's okay."

"What can I do for you?"

"I'm interested in a story I heard about from back East."

"The kid, right?" the man asked, with a knowing look on his feral face. He had a nose and hairline that brought to mind that kind of animal—a possum, maybe.

"That's right."

"What's your interest?"

"I heard they were traveling west; I'm traveling west. Maybe I'll spot something that will help. I'd like to know what the child looks like."

"Wait here."

The man opened the door and the noise of the press came rushing in. He left it open while he was gone, then returned with a copy of his own newspaper.

"We picked the story up from a Denver newspaper and reprinted it. Here it is, on the bottom of page one."

Clint took the newspaper and spotted the story.

"I have to get back to work," the man said. "You can have that."

"Thanks."

The man went back to his press, and Clint went outside, where he could read the newspaper in peace.

Since the little girl was missing from a town in Missouri and the story was from a Denver, Colorado, newspaper, the details were certainly not plentiful, but there was enough there. The girl's name was Diane; she was eight; and she was blond and habitually wore her hair in pigtails.

That was enough for him to want to get back to the camp and show the newspaper to Andrea. He'd be very interested to hear what she had to say.

TWENTY-FOUR

"So?" Andrea said.

"Is that all you have to say?" Clint asked. "So?"

"What do you want me to say?"

"I want you to tell me the truth, Andrea," Clint said. "Is Darlene actually this little girl, Diane?"

Andrea firmed her jaw and tightened her lips.

Clint had returned to the camp and had immediately taken Andrea to her wagon, away from the others.

"What's going on?" she'd asked, and he had thrust the newspaper into her face and made her read the story of the kidnapped girl.

That's when she said, "So?"

"Andrea," Clint said, "if Darlene is Diane, then people are looking for her. If that's the case, I can't help you."

"Why not?"

"Because it's just as if I helped you kidnap her," he said. "I could go to jail, and I'm not going to do that—not for you, or any of these kids. I'll help all

I can to get you to Ceremony, but not if that girl is kidnapped."

"After saying that you expect me to tell you that she is?" Andrea asked. "Do I look stupid?"

She was right. His diatribe had practically insured that she would lie. It was disconcerting to find that a seventeen-year-old girl might be more clever than he was.

"Okay then, let's put it this way," Clint said. "I think that Darlene and Diane are the same girl. For that reason I'm leaving."

"You can't!" she said, grabbing his sleeve as he turned to leave the wagon.

"Then tell me the truth."

"I can't," she said. "You'll leave anyway."

"Not if you tell me the truth."

"You won't go?"

"No."

"And you won't make her go back?"

"Yes, I will."

Andrea threw up her hands helplessly.

"You're not making this easy!"

"Is any of this easy, Andrea?" he asked. "Has any of it been easy up to now?"

She lowered her chin and said, "No," looking at her feet.

"Tell me what I want to know."

"All right," she said, after a moment. "Darlene is Diane."

"And Phil and Dave stole her?"

"What?" she asked, and then started to laugh.

"What's so funny?"

"Those two couldn't steal a child," she said.

"B-but you said they tried to steal one."

"And look what happened to them," she said. "No, no, I stole Diane."

"And how did you do that?"

"We sneaked her into the orphanage one night, and then she got into the wagons with us the next morning."

"And Dave and Phil didn't notice?"

"No."

"They don't sound very smart, those two gentlemen," he observed.

"Ha!" she said. "They weren't gentlemen, and they sure weren't smart."

"What do you mean, they weren't gentlemen?"

She hesitated a moment, then said, "Forget it."

"No, no, I want to know."

She stared at him.

"Did they—"

"Of course they did, Clint," she said. "God, sometimes men can be so naive. On two different nights they each tried to crawl under my blankets with me."

"They raped you?"

"No, of course not," she said. "I turned them away."

"How?"

"I told you, they weren't real smart," she said. "I made them believe they didn't want me."

"How did you do that?"

"Just by being smarter than they were," she said, "and that wasn't hard."

"You sound like you've had a lot of experience handling men, Andrea."

"I told you right from the beginning, Clint, I'm not a little girl," she said. "Men have been trying to touch me and have since I was twelve—and if your next question is, did some of them have me, the answer is yes. I haven't been a virgin for a long time."

"I-I'm sorry," he said helplessly.

"Oh, don't be sorry," she said. "I've learned a lot about handling men. About the only one I've ever found that I couldn't handle is you."

Now it was his turn to laugh.

"What's so funny?" she asked.

"You've done nothing but handle me since we met, and don't think that I don't know it," he said. "I'm not that naive, Andrea."

She smiled and said, "That's my point."

TWENTY-FIVE

"Wait a minute," Clint said. "We're getting off the track, here. Tell me how you came to sneak Darlene—I mean, Diane—onto the wagon, and why."

"The why is easy, Clint," Andrea said. "She wanted to come."

"Why?"

"Because her parents were mean to her."

"If every child who thought their parents were mean to them ran away, there'd be no kids left with their natural parents."

"Well, you know what I said Dave and Phil tried to do to me?"

"Yes."

"Well, that's what Diane's natural father was trying to do to her," Andrea said.

"What? His own eight-year-old daughter?"

"That's right."

How could a man think that way about any eight-year-old girl, let alone his own daughter? It was unthinkable. Of course, that was providing Andrea was telling the truth—this time.

"Andrea," Clint said, "are you telling me the truth?"

"If you don't believe me," Andrea said haughtily, "ask her."

The thought of asking an eight-year-old girl if her father was sexually interested in her did not sit well with Clint—and Andrea knew it.

She was still handling him.

"What are you gonna do, Clint?" she asked. "Are you gonna help us?"

"I'm going to think about it, Andrea," he said. "Meanwhile, I've got to go back to town."

"What for?"

"I sent a telegram and I need to see if an answer came in."

"Why did you come back?"

"I came back to talk about kidnapping."

"We didn't kidnap her, Clint," Andrea insisted. "She wanted to come with us."

"Well, that may be so, but her parents have called it kidnapping, and they reported it to the law, and there are people out looking for her."

"They'll never find us," Andrea said.

"Maybe," Clint said, "and maybe they will . . . and maybe those Comancheros will, too. And maybe nobody will. We'll just have to wait and see."

They both got out of the wagon, and Andrea grabbed Clint's arm.

"I'm sorry we lied to you, Clint," she said, "but I wasn't sure how you would react if we told you about Diane right away."

"Did Dave and Phil ever find out?"

"No, never." She tugged on his arm and asked, "Do you forgive me?"

He pulled his arm away from her and said, "No."

"Why not?"

"Because you want me to," he said. "You're trying to handle me again, Andrea, and I've got to wonder now how many more lies you've told me."

"Like what?"

"Like maybe the whole bunch of you are runaways."

"That's silly."

"Is it?"

He turned and walked to where he had left Duke. He couldn't even rest the big gelding. He wanted to see if an answer had come in from Rick. If someone was willing to take this bunch off his hands, then he was eager to find out that person's name.

Of course, he'd have to tell anyone who wanted the job about Diane. How anxious would they be for the job then?

TWENTY-SIX

Ray Jennings and the other Comancheros were ready to pull out when Con Able and Painted Man came walking up to the mounted group outside the livery stable.

"Thought you wasn't comin'," Jennings said to them.

"We're not," Able said.

"What?"

"Not now, anyway," Able amended.

"Why not?"

"I've got something to take care of here," Able said. "We'll catch up to you."

Jennings pointed a finger at Able and said, "If we catch up to them and take them, you don't get a share. Either one of you."

"That's okay, Ray," Able said. "I don't think there's anything to be had, anyway."

Jennings looked around, as if he was afraid the other men had heard him.

"Whataya talkin' about?"

"I decided that the wagons aren't worth chasing," Able said.

"Then why are you gonna catch up to us?" Jennings asked. "Why not just forget about it?"

"You'd like that, wouldn't you, Ray?" Able said. "No, I figure Clark and the other boys probably deserve to catch up to the wagons and get some of their pride back. I just want to be along to help."

"What's so important here, then?" Jennings asked.

"It's personal," Able said. "Don't worry, I'll catch up."

"I ain't worried," Jennings said. He wheeled his horse around and shouted, "Let's get movin'!"

Con Able and Painted Man stood and watched the Comancheros ride out, and then Able looked at the Indian.

"Don't say it," he said.

"I was not going to say anything."

"You were thinking."

"I am not allowed to think?"

Able just stared at the Indian and said, "Just don't make a habit out of it."

Tom Dewey watched from the window of his unofficial sheriff's office as all the Comancheros rode out except for Con Able and the Indian.

He moved away from the window and wondered why Able was staying when the rest were pulling out. Whatever the reason, it couldn't be good. He was going to have to keep an eye on Con Able and his Indian friend.

TWENTY-SEVEN

When Clint returned to Alston, he rode straight to the telegraph office. As Clint entered, the clerk looked up at him in surprise.

"Thought you left town."

"I did," Clint said, "but I'm back. Did I get a reply yet?"

"Sure did," the man said. "I was lookin' for you, but—"

"I understand," Clint said, cutting the man off impatiently. "Can I have it, please?"

"Sure," the man said, handing it over.

Clint took it outside to read it.

CLINT ADAMS ALSTON KANSAS
YOU GOTTA BE KIDDING STOP NO BABY-SITTERS
AVAILABLE STOP KIDS A HOT ITEM THESE DAYS
STOP READ THE PAPERS STOP SORRY CAN'T HELP
STOP WATCH YOUR BACK STOP

RICK HARTMAN
LABYRINTH TEXAS

Clint folded the telegram and shoved it into his pocket. Sure kids were a hot item when an eight-year-old girl is reported kidnapped. He'd know that if he made a habit of reading newspapers, but he didn't, not when he was on the trail, anyway.

So, he was stuck with Andrea, Eddie, and the little kidnapped Diane. What could he do with them other than take them where they were supposed to go? Once they were in Ceremony, California, they would be the problem of the people in that town.

Still, they were a long way from Ceremony.

Then a thought occurred to him. If the people of Ceremony wanted these kids badly enough, maybe they'd send somebody to get them.

He went back into the telegraph office.

"Somethin' wrong?" the clerk asked.

"Got another telegram to send."

"Write 'er down and I'll send 'er."

Clint took the paper and pencil and then stopped. How should he word this? What if the law was somehow taking a look at all telegrams that were being sent, and they saw this one talking about three wagon loads of kids?

He thought a moment, then came up with some wording he thought he could live with, even though he knew he was being paranoid.

"Okay," he said, handing the clerk the paper.

"Ceremony, California?" the clerk asked. "Never heard of it."

"Does that mean it doesn't have a telegraph office?" Clint asked.

"We'll find out, won't we?"

The clerk sat down and started tapping his key

while Clint waited. The clerk sat and waited for a reply, but one did not come.

"Looks like you're out of luck, friend," the clerk said. "Wherever this Ceremony is, it don't have a key."

Or, Clint thought uncomfortably, it didn't even exist.

"You know where I can find some maps?"

"Try the newspaper office."

The editor was surprised to see Clint back again.

"We didn't exchange names before," the editor said. The office was silent, and he seemed calmer. "Mine's Miller, Bud Miller."

"Clint Adams."

"Adams?" the editor asked. "*The* Clint Adams?"

"The only one I know."

"The Gunsmith Clint Adams, right?"

"I really don't have time, Mr. Miller—"

"How about an interview?" the man asked, as if he hadn't heard Clint at all.

"I can't—"

"Just a quick one."

"I need to see—"

"I just want to—"

"Miller!" Clint snapped.

The editor straightened and stared at Clint without blinking for a few seconds, as if he'd just realized who he was hounding.

"Uh," he said, "I didn't mean no harm."

"I know—"

"No offense—"

"None taken."

"I, uh, wouldn't be worth anything as a newspaperman if I didn't ask."

"I understand."

"You ain't mad?"

"No," Clint said, "I'm not mad."

"W-well then, what can I do for you, Mr. Adams?"

"I understand you have some maps here."

"Maps?" Miller said. "Why yes, I have many maps here."

"I'd like to see one."

"Which one?"

"A map of California."

"Sure," Miller said. "I'll bring it right in."

Clint waited while Miller left the office and came back with a rolled up map. He set it down on his desk and unfurled it.

"What are you looking for?" Miller asked.

"A town called Ceremony."

"You're in luck."

"Why's that?"

"I happen to have a very detailed map."

"Detailed enough to have a little town called Ceremony on it?"

"Let's see."

They bent their heads over the map together and, sure enough, came up with Ceremony.

"Looks like it's about a hundred miles south of Sacramento," Miller said.

"Thanks a lot, Mr. Miller."

"Are you, uh, sure about that interview?"

"I'm sorry," Clint said, shaking the man's hand, "I'm sure."

After Clint Adams left the office of the *Alston*

Ledger, Bud Miller sat down at his desk to assemble the facts he had. First, Adams came into his office and showed interest in a story about a kidnapped girl, and now he was interested in a town called Ceremony.

Well, Miller thought, rubbing his hands together, an editor as talented as he was ought to be able to make a story out of that.

TWENTY-EIGHT

Painted Man sat outside the whorehouse and waited for the trouble to start. One of two things would happen, he knew. Either someone would start screaming, or Con Able would simply come walking out with that look on his face, the look Painted Man had come to dread.

Able picked out a bosomy, dark-haired woman of about thirty and followed her up to her room. She was wearing high heels, stockings, and a revealing bustier. Her skin was creamy and smooth, and there was an abundance of bosom, which was what he liked.

Once inside she turned and asked, "How would you like it, honey?"

"I want you naked," he said, his breath coming heavy, "now."

"That's easy, honey," she said.

She removed her high heels and stockings and then her bustier. The garment had been tight and had left some red marks on her pale flesh.

"Don't worry," she said, rubbing her hands over the redness, "it'll fade away."

He wasn't looking at the redness anymore, though. He was staring at her full, slightly sagging breasts with their penny-brown nipples and wide aureola. Her thighs were heavy, but he liked that. The thatch between her legs was dark and bushy, and when she saw him looking at her down there she slid her hand down over her belly and began to finger herself.

"I'm wet for you, already, baby," she said. "Come on, how do you want it?"

Her eyes became heavy-lidded as she touched herself, and he knew he had chosen right. This one worked in a whorehouse because she liked sex.

"Rough," he said.

"Oooh, rough sex," she said. "You like that, huh, baby?"

"No," he said, sliding his bandanna off, "you do . . ."

"Wha—"

He clapped his hand over her mouth and then tied the bandanna around her head to muffle screams . . . because soon she would be screaming . . .

Able left the whorehouse and found Painted Man waiting outside with the horses. It was almost dark by now, but the Indian could still see Able's face, and saw that look.

"You have done it again," Painted Man said.

Able looked at him calmly and said, "Let's just mount up and ride, my friend."

Painted Man handed Able the reins to his horse and then turned and mounted his own. He would say nothing further about the incident.

Able mounted up, and the two men were about to leave when they saw someone standing in front of them.

It was Tom Dewey.

"Where you headed, Con?" Dewey asked.

"Thought we'd leave town now, Tom."

"Why now? Why so late? Why don't you wait until morning?"

"Thought we'd leave now," was all Able would say in reply.

"Well, I tell you what, Con," Dewey said. "Why don't you wait until I go inside that whorehouse and see what's goin' on?"

"There's nothing going on in there that's any of my business, Tom."

"Why don't you wait, anyway?"

Able stared at Dewey for a while, who was standing with his hands down at his side and his legs slightly spread.

"You alone, Tom?"

"Why are you asking, Con?"

Able shrugged his shoulders.

"Just curious, is all."

"Well, I expect I'll just let you find out for yourself if I'm alone or not. Why don't you and your friend dismount now and we'll go on inside."

Able shook his head.

"Can't do that, Tom," Able said. "Wish I could, but I can't."

"I'm sorry to hear that."

"Get out of my way, Tom."

Dewey shook his head.

"I can't do that, Con."

"Sure you can," Able said. "It's not like you're a real lawman or anything, Tom."

"I'm the law here, Con," Dewey said, "as much law as we have, anyway."

"Are we gonna do this?" Able asked.

"I think we both knew from the time you rode in that we were," Dewey said.

"Then let's do it," Able said, and drew his gun.

TWENTY-NINE

By the time Clint got back to the camp it was dark. Andrea was waiting for him by the fire. It was quiet enough so that he knew some of the children had gone to sleep already. As Clint rode up to the camp, Eddie stepped out from behind a wagon and pointed his rifle at him.

"It's me, Eddie."

"Oh, sorry, Clint."

"That's okay," Clint said. "You're alert. That's very good. Would you take care of Duke for me?"

"Hey, sure!" Eddie said.

"I picked up some supplies before I left town, too," he said. "They're in that sack hanging on the saddle."

"I'll take care of it."

He accepted Duke's reins and immediately began to talk to the big gelding.

Clint walked up to the fire.

"Hungry?" Andrea asked.

"Yes."

"All the others have eaten, but there's plenty left for you," she said. "I kept it hot."

"Thanks."

"And there's coffee."

"Good."

She handed him a plate of food and then a cup of coffee.

"So what happened?" she asked, sitting across from him. "Did you get anyone to take us off your hands?"

"No," he said. "Apparently, because of a kidnapping that happened back East, no one wants to take on any jobs that have to do with children."

"Oh," she said, looking at the ground. "Sorry."

"Are you?"

"Actually," she said, looking at him, "no, I'm not. Now you'll take us to Ceremony."

"I tried to get in touch with the people in Ceremony," Clint said. "I thought they might send someone out here to get you."

"They don't have a telegraph office."

"I found that out."

"So you're stuck with us, then?"

"It looks like it," he said. "I'm either stuck with you, or I can just leave the lot of you here and go off on my own."

"But you wouldn't do that, Clint," Andrea said. "Would you?"

"You know I wouldn't," he said.

"Yes," she said, "I know."

THIRTY

Con Able and Painted Man stopped riding about a mile out of town. The Indian dismounted and reached Able in time to catch the white man before he fell off his horse and hit the ground.

"Where's the bullet?" Painted Man asked.

"Left shoulder," Able said, obviously in pain.

"I will have to make a fire and then get the bullet out."

"All right."

Painted Man dragged Able away from the horses and settled him onto the ground, lying on his back. Next he got the man's bedroll from his saddle and put it behind his head. After that he gathered what he needed and built a fire.

"How bad is it?" he asked while his knife was lying in the fire.

"Not bad," Able said, but he was sweating, he had the chills. "What happened to Dewey?"

"You killed him with your first shot."

"Is this his bullet in my shoulder, or did he have help?"

"He had help, but that's his bullet."

"What about the others?"

"There were two," Painted Man said. "I killed them both."

"Good."

Painted Man tore Able's shirt, exposing the wound. First he washed it with water from his canteen so he could examine it. The edges of the wound were bright pink, and the blood was flowing slowly.

"Well?" Able asked.

"Not bad," Painted Man said.

"I told you that," the white man said. "Come on, get it out. We've got to catch up to Jennings and the others."

Painted Man retrieved his knife, which was now red-hot.

"This will hurt," he warned Able.

"Tell me something I don't know," Able said. "Just get to it."

Painted Man gave Able a piece of wood to bite down on and then worked on the wound with the hot knife. In the middle of the procedure, Able fainted. Painted Man proceeded to remove the bullet without having to listen to the other man grunt and curse.

"What happened to the girl?" Painted Man asked.

In his weakened state, Able answered rather than argue with him.

"She's dead."

Painted Man, sitting across from where Able lay wrapped in a blanket, looked at the ground and shook his head.

"I do not understand this urge you get to kill women," he said.

"Well, that makes two of us," Able said. "I don't understand, either."

"What does it feel like?"

"What, killing them? Or the urge to kill them?"

"I know what killing is like," Painted Man said. "What is the urge like?"

Able thought a moment, fighting hard to collect his thoughts.

"It's as if my head is growing," he said. "And if I don't . . . do it . . . my head will explode."

"And when you do it?"

"It's gone," Able said. "The urge is completely gone."

Painted Man stared at him.

"Don't look at me like that," Able said, annoyed. "When it happens, I pick women who won't be missed, don't I? They're just whores. It's not like they were real people, or something."

Painted Man didn't answer.

"I'm tired," Able said. "Wake me in the morning and we'll ride hard to catch up with the others."

"Why? You said yourself those wagons were not worth chasing. Why go after them? Why don't we just ride the other way, to California?"

"I told you, Painted Man," Able said. "The time is coming closer when I'll take command away from Ray Jennings."

Able pulled the blanket tighter around him. His bandaged shoulder itched and hurt.

"And then what?"

"Whataya mean, then what? Then we'll make some money. We won't be chasing down some group of wagons that have no value. We'll hit banks, trains, stages, whatever has money on it."

"We can do that without them."

"We can hit more places at the same time, collect three, four times the amount of money we would if we were working on our own. We talked about this, Paint. You agreed to try it this way."

"I did not know we would be chasing wagons into Kansas," Painted Man said, "or getting into shootouts in Manly."

"Maybe not," Able said, "but you knew you'd be making more money with me."

"We have not made any yet."

"Don't worry, my friend," Able said drowsily, "we will . . . we will . . ."

After Able fell asleep, Painted Man thought about his association with the man. Able had saved his life once, and he the white man's at least once. Did they owe each other anything after trading lives? What was it that bound him to this man? Why did he not just saddle his horse now and leave while Able slept?

He didn't know the answer to that. He did know that he was indeed bound to Con Able, somehow. He felt a loyalty to the man he'd never felt to anyone else. Aside from the occasional urge to kill a whore, Con Able was a good man, smart, and always in control.

Painted Man still couldn't understand Able's "urge" to kill. It was alien to him. He killed when he had to, to stay alive or to achieve his goal. He had never killed just for the pleasure of it—no, the need of it. That was what Able had. He didn't get any pleasure from his killing, but it filled his need.

How long, Painted Man wondered, would he be able to forget the women and keep riding with Able?

Would Able's urge to kill ever come when there were no women around? What would happen then, the Indian wondered, if it was only the two of them?

What then?

THIRTY-ONE

Since Ceremony was just south of Sacramento, the trip from Kansas would be virtually a straight line west through Colorado, Utah, and Nevada. Clint knew that they would have to be substantially outfitted for a trip like this, and he took this question up with Andrea.

"How much money do you have left from what Dave and Phil had?"

"I don't know," she said. "I'll have to go and count it."

"Okay, go ahead," Clint said. "Count it while we're getting ready to move out."

"Okay."

She ran to wherever she had the money stashed, and he set about getting the teams hitched up by the oldest of the other children, headed by Eddie. If they were going to be traveling together to California, everyone was going to have to know their job, even if the youngest of the children did nothing more than kick dirt over the fire to make sure that it was out.

Clint had made Eddie his second in command, which caused the youth's chest to puff out. He was walking around now, barking out orders to the other kids. Sam, the twelve-year-old, was giving him a hard time, but the others were obeying.

By the time Andrea returned from her count, two of the three teams were hitched up. Now that she was out of her wagon the kids started hitching the team to that one, as well.

"We've got almost a hundred dollars," she told Clint, who was surprised. If they had that much left, how much must Dave and Phil have started out with?

"That'll get us part of the way," Clint said. "I'll have to use some of my own money to get us the rest of the way."

"I'm sorry," she said.

He doubted it, but he said, "Don't be, Andrea. I got myself into this mess when I helped you against the Comancheros."

"Well," she said, looking off into the distance, "at least they don't seem to be coming after us."

"I don't know," Clint said. "They're a pretty vindictive bunch."

"What?"

"They like revenge," he said.

"Oh."

He kept forgetting she was seventeen, but every so often she did something to remind him. She was going to be incredible in a few years, hard for any man to resist—or outsmart.

They got all three wagons ready to go, and Clint agreed to allow Andrea to ride up front in her wagon, although he would not yet let her drive it. He didn't think she was strong enough, yet.

Clint mounted Duke, who had been saddled for him by Eddie. He would follow alongside the three wagons, while keeping a watch behind them. They still had the Indian pony, and he was considering letting Eddie ride it—when Andrea was strong enough to drive—to scout up ahead a little bit.

As for now he put Eddie on the lead wagon, and he rode up to it and said, "Okay, Eddie. Let's get started. We've got a lot of ground to cover."

"Right, Clint."

Eddie flicked his reins and urged his team to get started. The other two wagons followed. Clint brought up the rear for the first few miles before pulling up alongside the wagons.

It was going to be a long trip.

THIRTY-TWO

Ray Jennings looked down at the cold camp fire and then crouched down to hold his hand over it. Was there still some warmth there, or was it his imagination? That goddamned Painted Man would know in a minute.

"Hey, Clark?"

"Yeah?"

"Is there still some warmth here?"

Clark Day came over and held both hands over the ashes.

"I think so."

"Son of a bitch," Jennings said, standing up. "We wasted all that time in Manly when the whole time they were a few hours away from us."

Actually, there was no warmth left in the fire. Cunning Dog or Painted Man would have known that immediately. Clint Adams and the three wagons were more than half a day away by now, but Ray Jennings was so anxious for them to be closer that he convinced himself—and Clark Day—that they were.

"So who knew they'd stop at the first Kansas town they came to?" Day asked. "If I knew we were on the trail, I wouldn't stop. They're stupid."

"Yeah," Jennings said, shaking his head, "they're stupid."

He was stupid for listening to Con Able and stopping in Manly. If they'd kept on going, they would have run smack-dab into the three wagons, and this would all be over with now.

"What do we do now, Ray?" Day asked.

"Who's stupid?" Jennings asked him. "We follow them, what else?"

"They're headin' west," Day said, "probably to Colorado."

"So?"

"So I ain't never been to Colorado," Day said. "What's there?"

"The same thing that's here and in Texas, stupid," Jennings said. "People."

One of the other men, a young fella named Marcus Pell, came walking over. Pell, six feet tall and slender, was, at twenty-one, the youngest of the Comancheros, and had been with them the least amount of time. He had thought it would be exciting to ride with them, but lately he'd been having second thoughts. He hadn't seen them kill anyone yet, but the attack on the three wagons had scared him. The Indians—Cunning Dog and Painted Man—didn't like him because he had a red birthmark that covered most of his left arm. They thought it meant he had been touched by the devil. They never spoke to him, or ate near him, which suited him fine.

"Ray?"

"Yeah, what?"

"I don't think I want to go to Colorado, either," Pell said.

"Jesus Christ!" Jennings said, getting to his feet. "Byers?"

"Yeah?"

"You got any trouble going to Colorado?"

Byers frowned.

"No, why?"

"Carpenter?"

"Yo?"

"You goin' to Colorado?"

"I am if you are, boss."

"Anybody else got a problem goin' to Colorado?"

The other men shook their heads.

"How about further?"

"Further?" Clark Day asked.

"How much further?" Byers asked.

"Utah," Jennings said, "Nevada, hell, all the way to California if we have to."

"Why would we chase them all the way to California?" Pell asked.

Jennings grabbed Pell by the front of his shirt. The younger man was several inches taller, but Jennings outweighed him by a wide margin. When he pulled, Pell had no choice but to move.

"Because they'll go to California tellin' people how one man scared us away from them, that's why," Jennings said. "We don't want that, do we?"

"I guess not," Pell said, and Jennings released him.

"We're movin' out," Jennings said, and then looked

at Clark Day. "Any man who ain't comin' with us gets shot right here and now."

Day swallowed.

"I'm g-goin', Ray," he stammered, "I never said I wasn't."

"That's good, Clark," Jennings said, "that's real good. Mount up!"

"We better get moving," Con Able said to Painted Man. He sat up, as if to throw off the blanket that was around him, but he didn't have the strength.

"It is hours from dawn still," Painted Man said. "Go back to sleep. We can leave in the morning."

"We'll be too far behind by then," Able said.

"We will take a shortcut."

"What shortcut?"

"Do not worry," Painted Man said. "Go to sleep, and in the morning I will tell you something interesting."

Able settled down onto his back again and asked, "Why can't you tell me now?"

"Because," Painted Man said, "If I tell you now, you will forget in the morning."

"What do you—"

"Go to sleep," Painted Man said. "In the morning you will feel stronger."

"I ain't sleepy," Con Able said, then promptly fell asleep.

While Con Able slept, Painted Man felt no remorse over his intention to lie to the man. He was going to tell Able that the man who had saved the three wagons was Clint Adams. Indeed, Painted Man had gotten close enough to the wagons to see that and many things. He saw that the wagons were filled with children and no adults. He surmised, then, that there would be nothing in the wagons of any value to the Comancheros. Surely, when Ray Jennings and the others discovered this, they would kill everyone in those wagons. This did not concern Painted Man.

What did concern him was the presence of Clint Adams, the Gunsmith. When he saw this, he knew it was something that Con would want to know. Con would not be able to resist trying his luck with Clint Adams.

However, Painted Man had not said a word about it because he did not want Ray Jennings to know. He was waiting to get Able alone to give him the information. Unfortunately, Able's "urge" had gotten in the way, and then the shooting with Tom Dewey.

In the morning, he would tell Able about Clint Adams—and then he would lie. He would also tell him that Adams and the wagons were headed west, most likely to California. He would suggest that he and Able take a shortcut to intercept them in either Utah or Nevada, either place, before they could reach California. After that they would ride and rest and by the time Able realized they were not going to intercept Adams and the wagons, Painted Man would announce that since he was wrong in his assumption, he would now do whatever Able wanted them to do.

Surely, by this time, the wagons would be destroyed, and perhaps Clint Adams, as well. Or—if all the legends were true—Clint Adams would have disposed of the fifteen Comancheros who were now on his trail.

Whatever the case, Painted Man would have succeeded in tricking Able into abandoning his plan to lead the Comancheros by taking him on a wild-goose chase after the Gunsmith.

At this point in time, of course, Painted Man had no way of knowing that Clint and the wagons were indeed heading for California, and there was every likelihood that their paths would cross in Utah or Nevada, or even Colorado.

Painted Man was not a man who lied often, and in this case, his lie was unknowingly the truth.

THIRTY-THREE

Since the Comancheros did not have the services of Cunning Dog or Painted Man, they had a problem following the trail left by the wagons. They were killers—all but young Pell—not trackers, and much of the ground they were covering was hard-packed earth. For this reason they lost the trail more than once.

Meanwhile a story written by the editor of the *Alston Ledger* appeared and was picked up by other papers and reprinted. The reason for this was the headline on page one: CLINT ADAMS, THE GUNSMITH, AFTER KIDNAPPERS OF LITTLE GIRL.

An interview with—or story about—the Gunsmith was always news. Couple that with the story about the kidnapped little girl, and Bud Miller had himself a story other papers were anxious for.

One of the newspapers that picked it up was the *Jefferson City Star*, in Jefferson City, Missouri. Because it appeared there it was seen by one Eustice Bodine, whose friends all called him "Bo" because they were afraid to call him "Eustice."

Bo Bodine was a detective, and he had been hired by the parents of the kidnapped little girl, Mr. and Mrs. Gorman, to find their Diane. Bodine was traveling with two of his employees, Rat Taylor and Frank Gall. While they were technically detectives, their line of work involved more work with a gun—or brawn—than with their brains.

Bodine was a small man, well-mannered and even-tempered except when it came to his given name. He preferred to use his brain in the pursuit of his chosen profession and leave the rougher work to others. Hence his decision to bring Taylor and Gall with him.

Of course, if the need arose he could also use his fists or his gun just as well as the next man—and better than some.

At the moment Bodine was sitting in the Jefferson City Hotel dining room, reading a copy of the *Jefferson City Star*. Opposite him, each demolishing a heaping plate of steak and eggs, were Taylor and Gall.

"Well, well, well . . ." Bodine said out loud.

"What is it, boss?" Rat Taylor asked around a mouthful of eggs. He was called Rat because as a child he was always as filthy as one. His cleanliness as an adult was only slightly better.

"It looks like we have company," Bodine said.

"Where?" Gall asked, looking around.

Gall was the older of the two men, dirty blond hair receding from a weather-worn face that looked closer to fifty than the forty-three he actually was.

Rat Taylor was thirty-five, and if any of his childhood friends could see him now, they wouldn't call him "Rat." Taylor had grown up to be a strapping six five.

"Right here," Bodine said, "in the newspaper."

"What do you mean?" Taylor asked.

"Have either one of you ever heard of the Gunsmith?" Bodine asked.

"Who hasn't?" Rat Taylor asked.

"Who hasn't, indeed," Bodine said. "Well, some newspaper editor in a town called Alston, Kansas, says that the Gunsmith is looking for our little girl."

"If he finds her," Gall said, "instead of us, we don't get our bonus."

"I don't get my bonus," Bodine corrected him, "and you don't get paid."

"Yeah, right. Sorry, boss," Gall said, "you don't get your bonus."

"How do we stop him?" Taylor asked.

"Rat," Bodine said, his tone scolding, "if he can find the poor unfortunate little girl, why should we stop him?"

"Huh?"

Gall grunted, and Taylor looked confused.

"Whatever can be done to bring that poor girl home should be done."

"Yeah," Gall said, "by us."

"Let's not be heartless," Bodine said, touching his breast, "let's not think just of ourselves, but of the poor little girl."

"Who's probably dead by now," Gall said.

"I don't think so," Bodine said quickly, dropping his hand. "Remember, we know that two men were looking for children to take back home with them. What we don't know is where home was. I think she went with them."

"Went?" Gall said. "I thought she was kidnapped."

"That's what the parents call it," Bodine said, and didn't explain.

"What's this got to do with the Gunsmith?" Taylor asked.

"I'll tell you what it has to do with him," Bodine said. "He knows the West better than we do. If we find him, we'll find that child."

"What if he really ain't lookin' for the kid?" Gall asked.

"That's what we're going to find out," Bodine said. He folded the newspaper and put it down. "Eat up, boys. We're going to Alston, Kansas."

THIRTY-FOUR

During the trip Clint's main concern was the little girl, Diane. She was still going by "Darlene," though, and that's what the rest of the children called her, so that's what he called her.

He still didn't want to come right out and ask her about her parents—or her father, actually. Andrea had said it was the father who was... "touching" Darlene the way no father should touch his daughter. Clint had seen a lot of sick things in his life, but this was about the sickest thing he'd ever heard. In the end, if it turned out to be the truth, and the father had reported her kidnapped just to get her back, Clint was considering going to Missouri to horsewhip the father.

His experiences with Andrea to date, however, had taught him not to take her at face value. There was still the possibility that she was lying to him just to get him to help them, and not to turn Diane/Darlene back over to her parents.

They were in Colorado when Clint decided that his best bet to find out the truth was Eddie. The boy seemed controllable, which was probably what Andrea was doing to him, but he also seemed to be in need of a man's influence. Clint had caught Eddie more than once watching him, and on occasion emulating him. He'd watch him at night, sometimes, when the boy was on watch, and he would do the same things Clint did. He had even taken to drinking coffee. Also, he loved Duke. He was always talking to the big horse, and he touched him only when he saddled or unsaddled him for Clint. The boy seemed to know that there were only certain times the big gelding liked—or tolerated—being touched.

Eddie also wanted Clint to teach him to shoot. Clint had been putting him off, but in Colorado he decided maybe it was time for some lessons.

Andrea spotted Eddie as he was rushing to his wagon to get his rifle. As he came back past her she stopped him.

"Where are you going in such an all-fired hurry?" she asked.

"Clint's gonna teach me to shoot."

He started away, but she grabbed his arm and held it tightly.

"You're spending a lot of time with Clint, aren't you?" she demanded.

"What are you, jealous?" he asked, with a grin.

"No, stupid, I'm not jealous," she said harshly. "I just want you to be careful what you tell him, Eddie. Understand?"

"Sure, Andy," Eddie said, "I understand."

He shook her hand off and ran to meet up with Clint. As Andrea watched him go, she wondered if she was going to have to do something drastic to keep control of him.

Clint Adams was not a stupid man. She knew that he suspected her of still lying to him. He was making friends with Eddie in an attempt to get him talking.

She was going to have to do whatever it took to keep her hold over Eddie, and she didn't have guns and a big black horse at her disposal. She had only one thing—the thing she had been withholding from Eddie all the while just waiting for a time like this, when she needed it.

Eddie was going to get from her what he'd been wanting all along. Let Clint Adams try to compete with that.

Clint saw Andrea stop Eddie and watched the two of them talk. She was a smart girl; she knew what was going on. Eddie was about to get caught in a tug-of-war between Clint and Andrea, and it was a battle Clint was not sure he was equipped to win.

THIRTY-FIVE

Clint gave Eddie some pointers on firing his rifle, and in following them the boy's marksmanship immediately improved. While he instructed the boy, he asked him questions about Andrea.

"Where did you meet her?"

"In the orphanage."

"Did you grow up together?"

"In the orphanage we did."

"But not before?"

"No."

"How long were you in the orphanage again?"

"Since I was about five."

"Where did you come from?"

Eddie shrugged.

"I don't remember much about what happened before the orphanage."

"Did you get there before Andrea?"

"Yes," Eddie said. "She was older when she came, like thirteen."

"So she'd only been there about three or four years when you left?"

"That's right."

More instruction, more improvement, and then more questions.

"Where did Andrea come from?"

"Her family."

"She had a family?"

"She lived with an aunt and uncle," Eddie said.

"And what happened?"

"She said . . . her uncle wanted to, you know, touch her and . . . do things with her."

"And how did she get along with the other people at the orphanage?"

Eddie was about to answer, but then he stopped.

"What's wrong, Eddie?"

"I don't know if Andrea would want me to tell you these things."

Clint didn't want to press the boy, because then he might never open up again.

"All right, Eddie," he said, "we'll talk about something else."

"Do you think I'll be able to shoot like you one day, Clint?" Eddie asked.

"Better than me, Eddie," Clint said. "You're young, you've got a lot of time ahead of you to improve."

"What about as fast?" the boy asked. "Do you think I'll be as fast as you?"

Clint studied Eddie for a moment. None of the children had said a word to him about knowing who he was.

"What do you mean, as fast?" Clint asked.

Sheepishly, Eddie took a rolled up dime novel from his back pocket and handed it to Clint.

"You're the Gunsmith," he said.

Clint took the dime novel and glanced at it. It was one of many he had seen before, exaggerating his exploits, mostly so that the people back East could have something to read and get excited over.

"You've known who I am all along?" Clint asked.

Eddie nodded.

"What about Andrea?"

"No," Eddie said, "she doesn't know."

"Does anyone else know?"

Again, Eddie nodded.

"Who?"

"Sam."

"And no one else?"

"No."

"You two have been keeping this to yourselves? Just the two of you?"

"Yes."

"Why?"

Eddie shrugged.

"It's our secret."

Chosen like a true child, Clint thought. Sometimes he thought the most important thing to a child is a secret to keep, or to share with one other friend.

"Why haven't you told Andrea?"

Eddie made a face.

"She's real bossy, Clint," he said. "I don't know if you noticed."

"I noticed."

"I just, you know, want to have something that she doesn't know about."

"Like this?" Clint asked, handing back the dime novel.

"Yes," Eddie said, and tucked it back away in his pocket.

"Well, don't believe everything you hear, Eddie," Clint advised.

"Well, even if only half of it is true, it's still amazing."

Clint was about to correct the boy by telling him that nothing about him was amazing, that having a reputation wasn't all it was cracked up to be, but then he stopped and thought about it. Andrea had something he didn't have that she could use to keep Eddie's loyalty—and now, just maybe, he did, too.

"Well, some of it was amazing, yeah," Clint admitted, nodding.

"Can you teach me how to shoot a handgun?" Eddie asked anxiously.

"Do you have a handgun?"

"No."

"Well, when you have one I'll teach you how to shoot it."

"Well then, can you tell me some stories?"

"What kind of stories do you want to hear?"

"The kind that's in the dime novels," Eddie said, "but ones that really happened."

"I tell you what," Clint said, "I'll make a deal with you."

"What kind of deal?"

"I still want to know some more about the orphanage," Clint said, "and about Andrea. If you'll talk to me, I'll tell you some stories."

Eddie thought that over hard.

"You won't tell Andrea?"

"I won't tell her," Clint said. He put his hand on

the boy's shoulder, feeling deceitful, and said, "This will be our little secret, okay?"

Eddie thought about it a few seconds longer, biting his bottom lip, then nodded and said, "Okay."

THIRTY-SIX

Because Painted Man had never lied to him, Con Able believed his story about Clint Adams heading west with three wagon loads of children. It didn't make much sense to him, but he trusted the Indian, so it must be so.

Now they were in Colorado. Able's wound was healing nicely, and they were making good progress. Every so often Able would ask Painted Man if he saw any sign on the ground. Painted Man would say yes, but no sign of three wagons and one rider.

"We'll just keep heading west," Able would said, and Painted Man would nod.

Now they were riding along and Able suddenly said, "You know, you're right."

"About what?"

"About Jennings and the rest," Able said. "They really are an inept bunch. First they get chased off by one man, then we find out they were attacking three wagon loads of children. Now they're probably wandering around out there somewhere looking for them, and there's not a tracker among them."

Painted Man just nodded. He firmly hoped that was true, that Jennings and the rest were wandering around with no sense of direction. He also hoped they would wander over the edge of a cliff.

"How is your hand?" Painted Man asked.

"My hand's fine," Able said. He had experienced some numbness of his gunhand following his injury. Although he didn't say so, Painted Man was concerned that he might have done some damage with his knife when he was digging out the bullet.

"My shoulder's still stiff, though, but that will clear up in time."

Painted Man knew what "in time" meant. Able was determined that he'd be healed in time to face the Gunsmith and test himself against him. Personally, Painted Man doubted Able would be able to kill Clint Adams in a man-to-man showdown. He had killed Tom Dewey that way, but Dewey had put a bullet into him. Of course, Dewey was pretty fast, himself, but Painted Man had seen the Gunsmith in action once, years ago. That was how he had recognized him, even watching the camp from a distance. Once he knew the Gunsmith was the man who had chased off Jennings and his men, he was determined to keep Able away from him.

The odds of them crossing paths now were astronomical.

The trip from Jefferson City, Missouri, to Alston, Kansas, was quick because Bo Bodine and his men made most of it by rail. Bodine believed in travel by rail. It was more civilized than riding on horseback—and when someone else was paying the bills, it made more sense, too. Of course, to get to Alston from the nearest railhead required riding a horse, but he could put up with it for short distances.

Upon arrival in town he and his men went directly to the office of the *Alston Ledger* and asked to see the editor. Bodine asked for the man by name because he had seen it in the newspaper article he read.

"Bud Miller, at your service, gentlemen," Miller said. Of course over the din of the printing press it sounded to Bodine like he said, " . . . Mill . . . your ser . . . men . . ."

"Is there someplace we can go and talk?" Bodine shouted.

Miller held up a hand and then waved, indicating that Bodine should follow him.

"Wait for me in the saloon!" Bodine told his men.

Because of the press the only word they understood was "saloon," but that was all they needed to hear.

Bodine followed Miller into his office.

"Your telegram indicated that you were interested in my story about Clint Adams," Miller said.

Bodine had sent a telegram on ahead so that the editor would be prepared to talk to him.

"That's right," Bodine said. "I read your account in the paper, but I wanted to know what else Adams talked to you about."

"Well, there wasn't much else," Miller said. "He was real interested in that kidnapped girl. You've been hired to find her, you say?"

"That's right."

"You wouldn't be interested in an interview, would you?"

Bodine hesitated only a moment.

"After I find her, why not?" he asked. "I could use the publicity."

"Good, good," Miller said, rubbing his hands together.

"Think a minute, Mr. Miller," Bodine said. "Did he ask about anything else?"

"Well . . . there were the maps."

"Maps? What maps?"

"Well, one map, actually," Miller said. "He was interested in a map of California."

"California," Bodine repeated. "Why California?"

"Well, he was looking for a specific town."

"What town?" Bodine asked. "Do you remember?"

"No, not offhand—"

"What about if we looked at that map?" Bodine offered. "Do you think you'd remember then?"

"Yes, I might. . . ."

"Would you get that map, please?"

Miller went out into the din, leaving the door open behind him, and then returned with a rolled up map. He unfurled it and spread it out on his desk, as he had for Clint Adams.

"Now, what part of California was he interested in?" Bodine asked.

"He didn't really know," Miller said, frowning. "He looked all over for this small town until—wait, I think it was near Sacramento."

Bodine moved his finger over the map in the vicinity of Sacramento.

"Santa Lucinda?"

"No . . ."

"Del Vista?"

"No . . ."

"Ceremony?"

"No . . ."

"Buena—"

"Wait, wait," Miller said, "Ceremony, that was the one."

"Ceremony," Bodine said, touching it with his fingers. "I make that about a hundred miles south of Sacramento."

"Right."

So, Adams had some information about the girl that was sending him to Ceremony, California.

"Mr. Miller, thanks very much for your help."

"You won't forget about that interview, will you?" Miller asked.

"No, sir," Bodine said. "Once I have that girl back, I'll be in touch."

As Bodine left the newspaper office, Bud Miller was thinking that this was going to be a very good month indeed for his circulation.

Bodine found Gall and Taylor in the saloon and had a beer with them.

"Did you get what you wanted from the newspaper editor?" Gall asked.

"I did," Bodine said. "We're heading for California."

Taylor got a stricken look on his face.

"Not on horseback."

"Are you mad?" Bodine said. "We'll ride back to the railhead and catch a train. We'll be waiting for Mr. Clint Adams when he gets there."

"I'll drink to that," Gall said, raising his beer mug.

Bodine took the mug from Gall's hand and set it down on the bar.

"Drink to it in California. We're leaving now!"

THIRTY-SEVEN

Part of his strategy to get Eddie to talk to him was letting him handle his modified, double-action Colt. He unloaded it and handed it to the boy.

"What was Andrea like at the orphanage, Eddie?" Clint asked.

"She got whatever she wanted."

"Why was that?"

"Because the headmistress's husband liked her."

Eddie was turning the Colt over and over in his hand, then he held it and pointed it at the ground.

"Why did he like her?"

"Andy said he liked young girls."

"Did he ever . . . touch any of the girls?"

"I don't know."

"What about Andrea?" Clint asked. "Did she ever let him touch her?"

Eddie ducked his head and said, "No."

From watching the boy Clint had deduced that he would duck his head that way every time he was going to lie. That meant that Andrea had probably traded sexual favors at the orphanage to get what she wanted. She had been telling the truth about not being a virgin.

"Why did these children agree to leave the orphanage, Eddie?"

"Because they want homes, and families."

"Some of them are young enough that they would have been adopted sooner or later."

"They didn't want to wait," Eddie said. "Andy said—I mean, they wanted what Dave and Phil were offering, a town with no children where they'd be accepted."

"And what about you, Eddie?" Clint asked. "What do you want?"

The boy handed Clint back his gun and just shrugged.

"I don't know."

Clint had the feeling that Eddie wanted whatever Andrea told him he wanted.

"Eddie?"

"Yeah?"

"What's your last name?"

"Don't got one."

"You mean you don't know it?"

The boy shrugged.

"Don't remember."

"So what name do you use?"

"Just Eddie."

"And Andrea?"

"Same thing."

"And the other children the same?"

Eddie nodded.

"Whose idea was that?"

"Andrea's."

"That none of you would use last names?"

"Until we were adopted."

"What did you think of that idea?"

"Okay, I guess," the boy said, with a shrug.

"Do all the children listen to Andrea?" Clint asked.

"Most of them," Eddie said. "Sam's stubborn, but the others, they listen."

"And Sam? Does he listen to you?"

Eddie smiled then, and Clint had the feeling that Eddie loved Sam like a little brother.

"Yeah, he does."

"He looks up to you, doesn't he?"

"I guess."

"Eddie—"

"I gotta go, Clint," the boy said. "It's gettin' late and I gotta collect some more wood for the fire."

"Well, take your rifle," Clint said. "We'll have another shooting lesson tomorrow. How's that?"

"That's great!" Eddie said, picking up his rifle. "Thanks."

Clint watched the boy run back to camp and sat back to consider what he had learned about Andrea, Eddie, and the other children.

THIRTY-EIGHT

It was shortly after Bodine left Alston with Gall and Taylor that Ray Jennings and the Comancheros decided to go there. They had wandered aimlessly for days, trying to find tracks to follow, following false tracks, until one day Marcus Pell, the only Comanchero who could read, read a story in the newspaper about a man called the Gunsmith, who was looking for a missing child.

"Where's that newspaper from?" Jennings asked.

"The story was from Alston, Kansas."

"Alston?" Jennings said. "Isn't that where we found the camp?"

"Yes."

Jennings thought a moment, then punched the air and said, "That explains it."

"Explains what?" Clark Day asked.

"How one man could drive us off and make us think there were more."

Carpenter frowned and asked, "How?"

"It was him."

"Who?" Day asked.

"The Gunsmith... what's his name?" he asked Pell, pointing at him.

"Clint Adams."

"That's him," Jennings said. "Don't you see?"

Jennings was sitting near the fire with Day and Carpenter while the other men were scattered about, eating and drinking. Pell happened to pick up the newspaper in a nearby town they had passed through and had only now gotten the chance to read it.

"Wish I could read," Day said.

"I could teach you," Pell offered.

"Never mind that," Jennings said impatiently. "Don't you see, the man who was shooting at us had to be Clint Adams."

"So what do you want to do?" Day asked.

"I want to go to this town, Alston, and talk to this newspaper fella," Jennings said. "He can probably tell us where Adams is heading."

"You want to go after the Gunsmith?" Pell asked doubtfully.

"Why not?" Jennings asked. "There are enough of us to take him."

"What if you're wrong?" Carpenter asked. "What if you're wrong and we end up following the wrong trail?"

Jennings fixed the man with a baleful look.

"What trail are we followin' now?" he demanded. "This is better than nothin'. Besides, I'm not wrong. This makes sense."

Jennings stood up.

"Break camp," he said. "We're goin' to Alston."

Jennings walked away, and the three men looked after him.

"Think he's right?" Day asked.

"I don't know," Carpenter said.

"At least we're getting out of Colorado and back to Kansas," Pell said.

"Closer to Texas, anyway," Clark Day said, "that's all I care about."

"You want to go back to Texas, Clark?" Pell asked.

"I do. So do a lot of the others."

"I wonder what happened to Con," Pell said. He would rather have ridden with Con Able than with Ray Jennings any day. He'd hoped that Con would take over the Comancheros, and then he'd stay. Now he was still planning to leave, he just had to figure out a way to do it without Jennings killing him.

"Maybe once we're near Texas again Ray'll forget about those wagons," Carpenter said, "and we won't have to go traipsin' off after them again."

"I think it's crazy," Pell said.

The other two men stared at him.

"Well, I do," Pell said firmly.

Day and Carpenter exchanged a glance.

"Yeah, I do, too," Day said.

"You gonna tell him?" Carpenter asked.

"Not me," Day said.

"You?" Carpenter said to Pell.

"Nope."

"Then I guess we don't got much of a choice," Carpenter said, standing up. "Let's break camp."

THIRTY-NINE

It was several nights after his initial talk with Eddie that Clint decided to talk to Andrea. He waited until all the children were sitting eating dinner, then contrived to sit next to her while they ate.

This had been the first day she had driven one of the wagons since her injury.

"How do you feel?" he asked.

"A little sore," she confessed, "but otherwise fine. I'll be better tomorrow."

"Good."

He had gone over it in his mind and decided on an approach that wouldn't give away the fact that Eddie was talking to him in exchange for stories.

The stories. So far he had told Eddie stories of Bill Hickok, Bat Masterson, Wyatt Earp, Buckskin Frank Leslie, Fred Hammer—also known as the Black Gun—Ron Diamond—the Diamond Gun—and others he had ridden with. Eddie had listened to it all, and then asked questions in return.

It was clear now to Clint that Andrea controlled all of these children. What he didn't know was why.

"Andrea, can I ask you a question?"

"Why?" she asked. "Haven't you been getting enough answers from Eddie?"

"Eddie's pretty loyal to you. So are most of these kids."

"They like me."

"They respect you, too."

"I guess."

"They don't seem to have any last names," Clint said. "Why is that?"

"That's something we decided in the orphanage," Andrea said. "Some of us honestly didn't know our last names, others didn't want the ones we had. We decided that we wouldn't use any until we were adopted."

"Sounds like an idea that somebody in particular had to come up with."

She looked at him and then grinned. Suddenly, he thought she knew what he was doing, testing her to see if she would lie to him.

"You're right," she said, "it was my idea."

"How did you come up with it?"

"I gave up my last name years ago, and Eddie didn't even remember his," she said. "I don't know, it just seemed like a good idea at the time. How important can a last name be, anyhow?"

"It's real important to some people."

"Well, not to me."

"Did all of the children agree to go along with you on this?" he asked.

"No," she said, spreading her arms to indicate the children around them, "just these."

"I'll bet it acted as a bond between you, didn't it?" he asked.

"A bond?"

"Brought you all closer together?"

Andrea thought a moment, then said, "Yes, I guess you could say that. We're pretty close right now, aren't we? All of us?"

"I guess so," he said. She didn't seem to understand what he was trying to say, and he didn't push it. Maybe there was no bond between her and the children who were following her, maybe she just liked controlling them.

If that was the case, it would make her a different kind of person altogether.

Wouldn't it?

FORTY

The day the Comancheros rode into Alston they wasted no time. They rode down the main street, people scattering before them, and looked for the newspaper office.

"Hey you!" Jennings finally called out to a teenage boy.

"Me?"

"Yeah, where's the newspaper office?"

The boy turned and pointed and said, "Two blocks away, on your left, mister."

Jennings didn't say thanks; in fact he almost trampled the boy with his horse.

The Comancheros rode right up to the newspaper office and all dismounted.

"Wait out here," Jennings said. "Clark, you and Pell come in with me."

Pell was surprised. What had he done to deserve being included, he wondered, but he didn't argue.

"Hey, what if the sheriff comes along?" Carpenter asked.

"Just tell him we're inside buying a newspaper," Jennings said.

"And if he don't accept that?"

"Then kill him."

Carpenter nodded. That kind of order he could understand.

Jennings, Pell, and Day entered the office. The printing press was so loud they couldn't think.

"Shut that off!" Jennings told Day.

"I don't know how."

"Figure it out."

Day went over to the press. The man running it tried to get in his way, but Day just pushed him aside.

Bud Miller came out of his office and saw what was going on.

"Hey, what are you doing?" he demanded.

Somehow, Clark Day got the printing press to stop running and the room fell silent.

"Hey, you can't do that," Miller said to Day.

"I already did," Day said, with a smile.

"If you damaged that—"

"Never mind about that bein' damaged," Jennings said. "A lot worse could happen to you."

Miller looked at Jennings and said, "Who the hell are you?"

Jennings stepped forward and backhanded the little editor, snapping his head back and staggering him. Blood leaked from his bottom lip, which had been punctured by his teeth.

"That's the wrong way to talk to me," Jennings said. "Are you the editor of this paper?"

"Yes," Miller said, but it came out "Yeth," because his lip was swelling.

"Did you write the piece on Clint Adams?"

"I did."

"Good," Jennings said. He moved closer to the editor, who flinched.

"I ain't gonna hit you again unless you make me," Jennings said. "I just want to ask you some questions, and as long as you answer me we'll get along fine."

Miller waited for the questions.

"I want to know where Clint Adams is."

"Adams?" Miller asked. "I don't know where he—"

He stopped as Jennings poked him in the chest with two stiff fingers.

"Let's try this again," he said. "Where's Clint Adams, the Gunsmith?"

"I don't know," Miller said. But then he backed away from Jennings, holding his hands out in front of him and said, "But I can guess."

"It better be a good guess."

"Ceremony."

"Ceremony?" Jennings asked. "What the hell is that?"

"It's a small town in California," Miller said, "about a hundred miles south of Sacramento."

"What the hell is he doin' in Ceremony?" Jennings asked.

"I'm not sure," Miller said, "but I think he's looking for a kidnapped child."

Jennings turned to Pell who said, "That's what the story in the paper said, Ray."

"That's right," Miller said, "that's what I wrote."

"Why's he looking for some kidnapped kid?" Jennings asked.

"I don't know," the editor said, "but he was asking

about the child, and then asking about Ceremony. That's all I know."

"Is there a reward for this kid?"

"Yes."

"From where?"

"The East," Miller said, "somewhere in Missouri."

That Jennings could understand. Clint Adams was after the reward.

"Is that the truth?" Jennings asked.

"It's the God's honest truth, mister," Miller said. "Don't hit me again."

"I ain't gonna hit you, Mr. Editor," Jennings said, and as soon as Miller relaxed, Jennings drove his fist into the man's stomach. Miller dropped to his knees, gagging and fighting for his breath. Helpless, he thought in that moment that he was probably going to die because he'd fabricated a story about Clint Adams.

"Let's go," Jennings said to Pell and Day.

"What'd you do that for, Ray?" Pell asked.

"I felt like it, kid," Jennings said. "I don't need another reason."

After Jennings, Pell, and Day left the office of the paper, Miller got painfully to his feet and stared after them. Slowly, he was able to regain his breath, and the fear that had gripped him began to fade.

He was still alive.

He was glad they had accepted what he had said without asking any more questions. Now they didn't know that Eustice Bodine and his men were also headed for Ceremony. He hoped that these men would ride right into Ceremony in time to be killed by the detectives.

• • •

At that moment Clint Adams had no idea anyone was showing an interest in him. If anything, he had finally decided that the Comancheros had given up on finding the three wagons. He hadn't discounted their appearance entirely, but he wasn't as concerned about it as he once was.

He had been watching the children for days now and was starting to believe that they would be getting along fine even if he wasn't there. Sure, they needed him to save them from the Comancheros, but other than a situation involving violence he thought they would get along—with Andrea's direction.

Andrea, he decided, was like a mother to them. She treated them like her children, and they were all very respectful toward her. They obeyed her, almost blindly—all but Eddie. Clint watched the way Eddie looked at her, and he didn't see her as a mother. In fact, Clint thought they might be having sex—and he thought the development might have been recent. Maybe she'd been withholding sex from him until she thought it was absolutely necessary—and she thought the time was now.

He didn't like the idea of Eddie being caught in a tug-of-war between him and Andrea, and he decided that he would stop trying to use the boy to find out about the girl.

He decided he'd just ask her.

FORTY-ONE

"What do we do now?" Clark Day asked as they rejoined the other men outside.

"We're goin' to Ceremony, California," Ray Jennings declared.

"Huh?" Carpenter said. "What's goin' on?"

"I ain't never been to California," Marcus Pell said.

"All of us?" Clark Day asked. "Ray, you know how long a ride it is to California?"

"We ain't ridin'," Jennings said. "At least, we ain't ridin' horses."

"What are we ridin'?" Clark Day asked.

"The train."

"Huh?" Carpenter said again. "What's goin' on?"

"I ain't never rode no train," Marcus Pell said.

"What about the rest of the men?" Day asked. Maybe Jennings would let him stay behind with them.

"The rest of you can go back to Texas and wait,"

Jennings said. "The four of us can handle things in Ceremony."

"Just the four of us?" Day asked. "Against the Gunsmith?"

"Huh? What's goin' on?" Carpenter asked.

"Don't worry about the Gunsmith," Ray Jennings said. "I ain't never met a man yet who could stand up to a bullet in the back."

"In the back?" Day asked. He fervently wished he was going back to Texas with the rest of the men. Maybe they'd even run into Con Able. Day was starting to wish that Able had made a move to take over from Jennings a long time ago, then he wouldn't be going to California to try to shoot the Gunsmith in the back.

"Huh?" Carpenter asked. "Hey, what's goin' on?"

"I ain't never shot nobody in the back," Marcus Pell said.

Jennings slapped Pell on the back.

"Then it's time you learned how, kid."

Marcus Pell wasn't so sure he agreed with that. He thought fast, though, and figured once they got to California he could get lost pretty easy.

"Anybody don't want to come?" Jennings asked, eyeing them all menacingly.

They all shook their heads, and Carpenter added, "I wish I knew what was goin' on, though."

Clint finally decided to ask Andrea for the whole truth.

"What makes you think there's some truth that I haven't been telling you?" she asked.

They were in her wagon, away from the other kids who could be heard outside, playing.

"Isn't there?"

"Maybe," she said. "Maybe there is."

"But you don't want to tell me?"

"Maybe..."

"Maybe what?"

She paused, and he could see that she was thinking, possibly going over her options in her mind. Could she lie to him again and have him accept it?

"If there was something to tell," she said finally, "would you allow it to wait until we got to Ceremony?"

"Then there is something to tell?"

"Clint... I'm asking you to wait until we get to Ceremony. Would you do that for me?"

He hesitated, and she got the wrong idea. Before he could stop her, she had her shirt off and was naked to the waist. She had small breasts, well-shaped and firm, the breasts of a woman. Under other circumstances he might have been tempted.

"Clint..."

He picked up her shirt and tossed it back to her.

"Put it back on, Andrea," he said. "We'll wait until we get to Ceremony to talk about this again."

Con Able was starting to feel duped.

"Are you sure Clint Adams was heading for California?" he asked Painted Man.

"I am sure."

"We ain't come across him yet."

"Colorado is a big place," the Indian pointed out.

"Yeah, but if he was goin' in a straight line from Kansas to California—"

"Maybe he didn't go in such a straight line."

"And maybe he wasn't goin' to California, at all,"

Able said. "Maybe he stopped in Colorado, somewhere."

"Or maybe he is going to stop in Utah," Painted Man said, "or Nevada. You know, trying to cross his trail was a long shot anyway, wasn't it?"

Looking disappointed, Able said, "Yeah, I guess."

"Do you know what we need?" Painted Man asked.

"What?"

"A place to hole up and rest."

"And you got a place in mind?"

"Yes," Painted Man said, "in California. A place where a man can rest in peace and quiet, because there are little or no children."

Painted Man did not like children. He did not like talking to them, being around them, or, for that matter, killing them. It was another reason he had steered Able away from the three wagons.

"Okay, then," Con Able said, "where is this wonderful place?"

"It's a little town south of Sacramento," Painted Man said, "called Ceremony."

FORTY-TWO

The first to arrive in the little town of Ceremony were Bo Bodine and his two men, Gall and Taylor. They had taken the train to Sacramento, where they rented horses and rode the hundred miles south to the town Clint Adams had shown an interest in, in Alston.

They rode in, left their horses at a nearby livery stable, checked into a hotel, then went walking, looking at the town and ultimately ending up in a saloon.

"Have you noticed anything about this town?" Bodine asked, over a beer.

"It's small," Gall said.

"But busy," Taylor added.

"What else?"

"No telegraph office," Gall said.

"I noticed that, too," Taylor said.

"What else?"

"Pretty women?" Gall asked.

"I didn't notice that," Taylor said.

"Neither did I," Bodine said, "but I did notice that there were no children."

"No children?" Gall asked.

"I didn't notice that," Taylor said.

"That's why I'm the detective," Eustice Bodine said.

"When do you think Adams will get here?" Gall asked.

"Maybe not for days," Bodine said.

"What do we do in the meantime?" Taylor asked.

Bodine looked at both of them and said, "We'll just have to wait."

Everything changed after Clint's talk with Andrea. There were no undercurrents during the trip, no tug-of-war with Eddie in the middle. The boy was free to spend time with Clint, with no danger of saying the wrong thing. It was understood that whatever there was to be explained would be explained in Ceremony.

He continued to teach Eddie how to shoot. He also spent some time with Sam. It was odd, but he felt that it was these two boys who most needed the influence of a man. Andrea knew it, too. Often when he was spending time with either boy he would catch her watching them, and she looked satisfied and happy.

Like a mother.

FORTY-THREE

Second to arrive were the four Comancheros, two days later. Ray Jennings, Marcus Pell, Day, and Carpenter arrived in Sacramento, rented four horses, and rode to Ceremony.

"It's small," Pell said as they rode in.

"That's good," Jennings said. "Adams won't be hard to find."

"I ain't never been this far west," Carpenter said.

"Me, neither," Pell said.

Pell wasn't happy. He had not been able to get away from the other men in Sacramento, and now Ceremony was too small for him to get lost in.

"Let's get over to the livery and take care of these horses," Jennings said. "I want to get a beer and take a look at the town."

"What if he's here already?" Day asked.

"How could he be, stupid?" Jennings asked. "We took the train to get here, he's ridin' a horse—plus he's got three wagons with him."

They started riding for the livery.

"I ain't never been on a train before," Carpenter said. "I didn't like it."

"Why not?" Day asked.

"It ain't natural, that's why."

"You think ridin' horses is natural?" Jennings asked. "Some man came up with that, too, just like the train."

"What about robbin' trains?" Day asked. "Ain't you ever done that?"

"Naw," Carpenter said, "I used to stick to stagecoaches and banks. Hey, Ray?"

"Yeah?"

"Think we could ride back to Texas?" Carpenter asked. "Or take a stage?"

"We'll take the train back," Jennings said.

"We got enough money?" Day asked.

"We'll have the reward money we get from Adams."

"What if he don't find the kid?" Day asked.

"Then we'll kill him and do it Carpenter's way. We'll ride back."

"Ray, want me to take the horses to the livery?" Pell asked. He didn't want to go back to Texas by train, stage, or on horseback. Maybe if Jennings let him take the horses to the livery he could drop off their three and then just ride off.

"Naw, we're probably almost there—yeah, see? There it is."

Pell saw it, and his heart sank. When was he going to get the chance to get away?

FORTY-FOUR

Rat Taylor was sitting out in front of the saloon when the Comancheros rode in. If there was one thing he knew on sight, it was bad news, and these four were bad news—except maybe the young one. He just looked scared.

After they had ridden by he got up and went inside. Bo Bodine had been spending most of the past two days sitting at a table by himself, nursing a beer and playing solitaire, but right now he wasn't there.

Frank Gall had found himself a three-handed poker game.

"Frank?"

"Hmm?"

Taylor stood behind Gall and saw that he was holding three jacks in his hand. Maybe his friend's luck was about to change.

"Where's Bo?"

"Wait a minute, Rat," Gall said. He picked up

some chips and tossed them into the pot. "Call the raise. Whataya got?"

The man seated across from him spread his cards to reveal his hand, three queens.

Maybe his luck hadn't changed.

"Shit," Gall said, throwing his hand in.

"Frank?"

"Yeah, what?"

"Where's Bo?"

"Upstairs," Gall said. "Where else would he be?"

That's where Bo Bodine was when he wasn't nursing a beer and playing solitaire, upstairs with a girl named Lila.

Bo Bodine looked down at the dark hair of the whore, Lila, her head bobbed up and down in his lap. The girl had his rigid penis trapped in her mouth, but it was a damp, velvet-lined trap. He reached down to cup her head in his hands and slow down the sliding motion of her lips and the sucking motion of her mouth. She released him, and smiled lasciviously then slid up and sat on him, taking his penis inside her. Her pussy was hot and wet on him, and he laughed and reached for her small breasts. She smiled again, her broad mouth revealing white teeth. Lila was slender, with little, perfectly formed breasts that had large, distended nipples. He palmed them, then touched them with his thumbs . . . and then there was a knock on his door.

"Don't move," he told her. "Come in."

The door opened and Rat Taylor walked in. He stopped short when he saw the naked whore sitting astride his boss. Of course, he could only see her from behind, but what he saw froze him. Slender shoulders, long black hair against pale skin, the long line of her back as it swooped down to the cleft between her buttocks.

"Bo?"

"Yeah?" Bodine peeked around from behind the girl's body. "I'm here. What is it, Rat?"

"Bads news."

"How bad?"

"Four Comancheros just rode into town."

"So?"

"I got a bad feeling."

Lila started to shift her weight, but Bodine held her by the hips and said, "Don't move, Lila. What are you saying, Rat?"

"Just that these fellas rode into town, and they look like bad news."

"Well, this town's got a sheriff, don't it?"

"Not that we've seen."

Bodine frowned. That was true. Although they hadn't gone out of their way to meet the law in Ceremony, neither had they seen him walking around town. He wondered about that.

"Does this town have a sheriff, Lila?"

"I guess."

"You don't know?"

"I try to stay clear of the law, Bo," Lila said.

"Well," Bodine said, stroking her right breast, "I guess I can understand that."

"Bo?"

Bodine looked at Taylor.

"Rat, go down to the bar, have a beer, and engage the bartender in conversation."

"About what?"

"About the law in Ceremony," Bodine said. "Find

out if it exists, and if so, how many men it consists of. Can you do that?"

"Sure I can do that, Bo," Taylor said. "All it is, is talkin'."

Bodine watched Rat Taylor walk to the door and leave, knowing full well that talking was not one of the man's strong points.

He knew Frank Gall was downstairs playing poker, and that wasn't one of Gall's strong points, either.

Both men did have strong points, though. They were tough, they did what they were told, and they had the ability to recognize trouble when they saw it. Bodine put a lot of stock in what Rat Taylor had just said. He had no doubt that four men had ridden into town looking like bad news to him. He just hoped there was enough law in Ceremony to handle it. The one thing he didn't want to do while waiting for Clint Adams to arrive was attract undue attention. That was why he was either downstairs playing solitaire and nursing a beer, or up here with Lila.

"Is he gone?" Lila asked.

"He's gone."

She began to ride him then, but as she did he found himself distracted. Even as his body responded to hers, his mind was wondering how much longer he was going to have to stay here. The longer he stayed in one place, the more chance there was of running into trouble. It was his history that if he stayed in one place too long trouble reared its head, and even when it wasn't his trouble he found himself involved in it.

He hoped that Clint Adams would arrive before that happened here.

FORTY-FIVE

Jennings, Pell, Day, and Carpenter left their horses off at the livery and checked into the hotel, getting two rooms. Jennings wanted four, but they didn't have four available.

"What the hell kinda hotel is this?" he demanded.

"I'm sorry, sir," the clerk said, obviously frightened, "but we only have two rooms available."

"Shit," Jennings said. He looked at Pell and said, "You'll bunk in with me, kid."

Pell swallowed and said, "Sure."

They got the keys to the rooms but didn't go up.

"Let's get a drink and see what this town's like," Jennings said.

Day and Carpenter knew what that meant. They had been with Jennings a lot longer then Pell.

As they followed him out of the hotel, Day said, "Shit, not again."

"I know," Carpenter said.

"What?" Pell asked. "What is it?"

Day looked at him and said, "He's got that look in his eye."

"What look?"

"He's gonna want to take over the town," Day said.

"What?" Pell said. "Take over a whole town?"

"It's easy," Day said, "he's done it before."

"Yeah, but just the four of us?" Pell asked.

"Maybe he won't do it," Day said.

"Let's see what happens in the saloon," Carpenter said. "That'll tell the tale."

When Bodine came down to the saloon, he bought himself a beer and sat down at the same table he'd been sitting at for the last two days and dealt out a game of solitaire. After a moment Rat Taylor came walking over and sat across from him. Frank Gall was still playing poker and, from what Bodine could see, was still losing.

"Frank really should try a new game," Bodine said. "What did you find out about the law?"

"The bartender says there's a sheriff, but he ain't worth much," Taylor said. "He says the town's looking for a new one."

"Great," Bodine said, shaking his head. "Have you seen those Comancheros again?"

"No, not yet."

As if on cue, the batwing doors opened, and four men walked in.

Bo Bodine knew trouble when he saw it, too.

"Oh, great."

FORTY-SIX

Jennings walked to the bar and demanded four beers. He didn't order them, he demanded them. Day, Carpenter, and Pell all followed. Day and Carpenter were looking around the place, checking to see who would be trouble if Jennings decided to make a move. Pell was just looking around for a way out.

"Come on, come on," Jennings said, "come on with those four beers."

It was still afternoon, so there weren't that many customers in the place. Other than the table where the three-handed poker game was going on and the one where Bodine was sitting with Taylor, there was only one table occupied. A couple of men stood at the bar.

"It's about time!" Jennings said. He reached for the beer before the bartender had put them all down and knocked one out of the man's hand. The beer went all over Jennings.

"Goddamn you!"

"Hey, you did it," the bartender said.

"Son of a bitch."

Day said, "Ray, take it easy."

"I'll kill the son of a bitch!" Jennings said, wringing his hands and spraying beer around.

Across the room Bo Bodine was watching what was going on and hoping against hope that it wouldn't develop any further.

"Boss—"

"Don't even think it, Rat," Bodine said. "We're not getting involved."

"Boss—"

"I said forget it."

"Boss," Taylor said urgently, "look at Frank."

Bodine looked over at Frank Gall, who was sliding his chair back and getting up.

"Jesus," Bodine said. "Great."

"Ray, don't—"

Jennings started to draw his gun, and Marcus Pell just knew his boss was going to shoot the bartender.

"Hey!" Frank Gall shouted. "Drop it!"

"Damn," Day said, and went for his gun. He knew Carpenter would be doing the same thing. They were going to have to back Jennings's play.

Marcus Pell hit the floor.

Bodine stood up, kicking his chair away. Rat Taylor did the same, drawing his gun and turning to face the bar.

"Hold it! Hold it!" Bodine shouted. He hoped to

keep even one shot from being fired, but he knew he was too late.

The first shot was fired by Ray Jennings, and it struck Frank Gall in the hip. Gall had his gun out and as Jennings's bullet hit him, he pulled the trigger. His bullet hit Clark Day in the knee, shattering it. Day went down, almost falling on top of the prone Pell.

Bodine fired, and his bullet hit Jennings in the shoulder.

Jennings fired, and his shot went wild, into the ceiling.

Rat Taylor aimed and shot Carpenter in the chest, killing him instantly.

From one knee Jennings angrily fired, his bullet hitting Rat Taylor in the right thigh.

Bodine fired again, and this time his bullet struck Jennings in the throat. When he fell, he landed on Pell.

Marcus Pell yelled and rolled free of Jennings's body.

He got to his knees and saw Bodine pointing his gun at him.

"Hey, no," Pell shouted, "don't shoot!"

"Toss your gun away, son," Bodine said. "Use your left hand."

Pell did as he was told, dropping his gun to the floor with his left hand.

"Frank?" Bodine called out.

"It's just my hip, Bo," Gall called out, struggling to his feet.

"Check those Comancheros. Rat?"

"My thigh," Taylor said. Bodine could hear the

pain in his tone. "I'm okay."

"This one's still alive, Bo," Gall said, pointing his gun at the wounded Clark Day. "The other two are dead."

"What about you, boy?" Bodine asked. "What's your part in this?"

"Honest, mister," Pell said, "I been looking for a chance to get away from them."

"You don't look like one of them, son," Bodine said. "What were you looking for, excitement?"

"I—I guess."

"Have you had enough excitement?"

"Oh, yeah."

"Then get going before the law gets here."

"What?"

"Go."

"My gun—"

"Go . . . now!"

Pell didn't hesitate. He ran from the saloon, grateful for the chance to finally be free. The last anyone saw of him he was heading for the livery stable. . . .

"Now what?" Rat Taylor asked Bodine.

"This is what I didn't want," Bodine said. He looked at Gall and scolded, "Frank!"

"I couldn't just let him kill the bartender."

"Shit, why not?" Bodine said, but he knew he couldn't have let it happen, either.

"What now?" Taylor asked again.

"Now we wait here for the sheriff," Bodine said, "then get you and Frank to the doctor, and then we continue to wait for Clint Adams. In other words, business as usual."

FORTY-SEVEN

It was three weeks before Clint Adams and the wagons arrived in Ceremony.

The wounds Rat Taylor and Frank Gall had suffered during the shoot-out with the Comancheros in the saloon had almost healed. The sheriff, who had arrested Clark Day and put him in jail, promptly resigned, leaving the office vacant. The town council had offered the job to Bo Bodine and had, in fact, been doing so on an almost daily basis since the shooting.

Bodine explained that he was simply in town waiting for someone to arrive.

"That's strange," Matt Sinclair, the head of the town council, had said. "We're waiting for some people to arrive, too."

"Well," Bodine said, "I'm sure it's not the same people."

"Perhaps not," Sinclair had said. "Mr. Bodine, are you sure you won't take the job?"

• • •

When they came within sight of Ceremony, Clint called the little wagon train—he'd taken to calling it an "Orphan Train"—to a stop.

"Is that it?" Eddie asked. "Is that Ceremony?"

"That's it."

Andrea came running up to them.

"What's wrong?" she asked.

"That's it, Andy," Eddie said. "That's Ceremony."

"You mean we made it?" she asked.

Clint nodded.

"We made it."

"It's small," she said.

"I've seen smaller."

"Now what?" she asked.

"Now let's get into town and see who we have to talk to about getting these kids some parents."

Andrea got back up on her wagon, and they started for town.

Clint soon found out that he didn't have to seek anyone out. As soon as he and the wagons appeared on the street, they were mobbed by people who had been waiting for them to arrive.

"Where are Dave and Phil?" someone asked.

"Who are you?" another person asked.

"Where are the children?" a woman asked.

"Who do I talk to?" Clint asked.

He had to ask the question a few times before a man stepped up and said, "Talk to Matt Sinclair."

"Where is he?"

"Follow me."

Some of the children stuck their heads out of the wagons to look, and the people went crazy.

"Oh, look how adorable . . ."

"How cute . . ."

"I want that one . . ."

Clint followed the man who was on foot to the building where this Matt Sinclair had his office, with the wagons following him.

"This is where his office is," the man said.

"Could you get him for me, please?"

"Sure."

Clint dismounted, and the children started coming out of the wagons and gathering around him. They were all in turn surrounded by the townspeople, so that by the time Sinclair came out he had to push his way through to Clint Adams.

"Are you Sinclair?" Clint asked.

"That's right, I'm Sinclair," the man said. "Who are you, and where are Dave and Phil?"

"My name is Clint Adams, Mr. Sinclair," he said. "Your two men were killed some months back, it seems."

"And how did you end up with these children?" Sinclair asked.

"It's a long story. Is there somewhere we can talk?"

"My office," Sinclair said. "Follow me."

"Can someone look after these children?" Clint asked.

"They'll be taken care of," Sinclair said. "We've been waiting a long time for them."

"Uh, before we go inside . . ." Clint said. He turned and called out, "Andrea!"

Andrea came to his side.

"This is Andrea," Clint said. "I think she should come inside with us. She's the oldest. She'll be able to tell you what happened to your men."

"All right, then," Sinclair said. "Let's go inside."

As they entered the building, Clint whispered to Andrea, "Now's the time."

"For what?"

He looked at her and said, "For the truth."

FORTY-EIGHT

"Say that again?" Matt Sinclair asked. "Please?"

Clint had already told his story about how he came to be the children's escort, and now Andrea was telling the story of how Dave and Phil died. Clint was hearing the real story for the first time.

"I said," Andrea repeated, "Dave killed Phil, and we killed Dave."

Sinclair couldn't believe it.

"What do you mean, you killed Dave? Why? And why would he kill Phil?"

"Because Phil was trying to stop him."

"From doing what?" Sinclair asked.

Andrea looked at Clint, and he nodded.

"From raping me."

"What?" Sinclair said.

"That's right," she said. "One night Dave came into my wagon and started talking to me . . . and putting his hands on me . . . under my clothes . . ."

Clint knew things about Andrea that Matt Sinclair

didn't, and he was thinking, Good God, let her be telling the truth this time.

"Phil heard me shouting, and he came running. He got in a fight with Dave. Dave hit him, and Phil fell and hit his head. He was dead."

"What happened then, Andrea?" Clint asked.

"Dave said it was my fault that he killed Phil, and that I had to pay. He—he started ripping off my clothes."

"And?" Sinclair asked.

"The children tried to stop him, but he was too strong. Finally . . . finally Eddie shot him."

"Eddie . . ."

"He's the oldest of the boys," Clint said.

"My God!"

"One shot didn't kill him, though," Andrea said, "and Eddie couldn't shoot him again, not when he was already wounded."

"And?" Sinclair prodded.

"So I did," she finished. "I'm the one who really killed him."

Sinclair sat in stunned silence.

"Mr. Sinclair, was Dave a family man?"

"No," Sinclair said, "we just hired him to go with Phil. Phil had a family here in town. I'll—I'll have to tell them."

"Tell them that he was a good man," Andrea said. "He tried to help me."

For the first time Sinclair smiled and said, "I'll tell them."

"Oh, there's one more thing," Clint said to Sinclair.

"Now what?"

"One of the children has been reported kidnapped."

"Kidnapped?"

Clint nodded.

"Sweet Jesus," Sinclair said, "tell me about this one."

After Andrea finished telling the story about Diane/Darlene, Sinclair asked her, "Is this true? Her own father?"

"You can ask her," Andrea said.

"Oh, I'll ask her," Sinclair said, "and I'll also start an investigation to see if it's true. This town has been starved for children for so long, and here's a man who . . . who does that to his own daughter?"

There was a knock at the door at that moment, and Sinclair called out, "Come in."

The door opened and a man of diminutive height entered.

"Excuse me, but I'd like to talk to you, Mr. Sinclair."

"Mr. Bodine," Sinclair said, "come in, come in. Have you reconsidered our offer?"

"No, I haven't, but it would seem that the man you were waiting for is also the man I was waiting for," Bodine said, looking at Clint Adams. He extended his hand and said, "Eustice Bodine, Mr. Adams."

"Mr. Bodine," Clint said, shaking the man's hand shortly and then releasing it. "I've heard of you. What does a detective want with me?"

"I'm looking for a little girl," Bodine said, "who was kidnapped from her family in Missouri. I understand you're looking for her, too."

A silence fell over the room.

"Actually," Clint said finally, "I wasn't looking for

her at all, but as it happens I do know where she is."

"Well, if you'll let me have her, I'll return her to her parents. I won't even ask how you happened to—"

"Mr. Bodine," Sinclair said.

"Yes?"

"I think you'd better sit down," Sinclair said. "There's something you should hear."

FORTY-NINE

Several days later Clint and Bodine were talking in the saloon. The children had been taken to the town hall, where the town would begin its own adoption proceedings that day. Clint didn't feel he had to be there to see that. He had been staying at the hotel as a guest of the town and had not been charged for a meal or a drink since arriving.

"You know," Bodine said, "if this turns out to be true, I'm going to be a little disappointed in my own judgment of character. The parents—especially the father—seemed real concerned."

"Well, if you satisfy yourself that it's not true," Clint said, "the girl will still be here."

"Oh, I'll look into it," Bodine said.

"I still can't get over the coincidence of those Comancheros getting into a shoot-out with you."

"Not such a coincidence, if they were here looking for you. They just happened to arrive too early, not realizing, I guess, just how far ahead of you the train had gotten them here. In fact, I hadn't realized it, either. Anyway, I'm ready to leave this town."

"I thought they wanted to hire you as sheriff," Clint said.

"They do, but that's not a job for me. One of my men might take it, though. They're talking to Sinclair now."

"When will you be leaving?" Clint asked.

"Tomorrow."

"Me, too."

"I'll be riding to Sacramento to catch the train," Bodine said.

"I'm going to Sacramento, too," Clint said. "I have friends there. Maybe we can ride together."

"Sure," Bodine said, "why not?"

Clint finished his beer and then stood up.

"I have to go and say good-bye to some people," he said.

"The kids?"

Clint nodded.

"Get attached to them, did you?"

"Yeah, kind of."

"I understand Sinclair and his wife are going to adopt the girl, Andrea, themselves."

Clint shook his head and said, "I wish them luck. She's a handful. They're also going to take Eddie. They wanted older kids."

That would make Eddie and Andrea brother and sister, sort of. Clint had never found out for sure if the two were having sex, but if they were, it was going to make for an interesting household.

"Well, good luck with your good-byes," Bodine said. "I'll walk out with you."

Clint and Bodine left the saloon, passing two men who were on their way in. One was an Indian who looked at Clint strangely as they passed.

"I thought you said this town didn't have no kids?" Con Able complained to Painted Man.

"It didn't the last time I was here."

"Well, it's got a ton of them, now."

"We'd better keep moving then," Painted Man said.

Able ordered a beer and shook his head.

"I can't believe we didn't cross paths with the Gunsmith, or catch up to him yet."

"Don't worry," Painted Man said. "When I see him, I'll know him. Let's have that drink and keep on moving."

Watch for

THE MAGICIAN

155th in the exciting GUNSMITH series
from Jove

Coming in November!

If you enjoyed this book, subscribe now and get...

TWO FREE

A $7.00 VALUE—

If you would like to read more of the very best, most exciting, adventurous, action-packed Westerns being published today, you'll want to subscribe to True Value's Western Home Subscription Service.

Each month the editors of True Value will select the 6 very best Westerns from America's leading publishers for special readers like you. You'll be able to preview these new titles as soon as they are published, *FREE* for ten days with no obligation!

TWO FREE BOOKS

When you subscribe, we'll send you your first month's shipment of the newest and best 6 Westerns for you to preview. With your first shipment, two of these books will be yours as our introductory gift to you absolutely *FREE* (a $7.00 value), regardless of what you decide to do. If you like them, as much as we think you will, keep all six books but pay for just 4 at the low subscriber rate of just $2.75 each. If you decide to return them, keep 2 of the titles as our gift. No obligation.

Special Subscriber Savings

When you become a True Value subscriber you'll save money several ways. First, all regular monthly selections will be billed at the low subscriber price of just $2.75 each. That's at least a savings of $4.50 each month below the publishers price. Second, there is never any shipping, handling or other hidden charges—*Free home delivery*. What's more there is no minimum number of books you must buy, you may return any selection for full credit and you can cancel your subscription at any time. A TRUE VALUE!

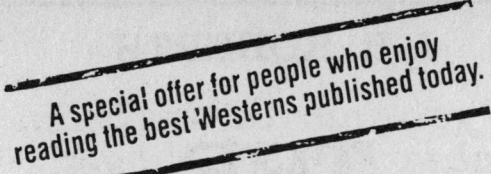

A special offer for people who enjoy reading the best Westerns published today.

WESTERNS!

NO OBLIGATION

Mail the coupon below

To start your subscription and receive 2 FREE WESTERNS, fill out the coupon below and mail it today. We'll send your first shipment which includes 2 FREE BOOKS as soon as we receive it.

Mail To: **True Value Home Subscription Services, Inc. P.O. Box 5235 120 Brighton Road, Clifton, New Jersey 07015-5235**

YES! I want to start reviewing the very best Westerns being published today. Send me my first shipment of 6 Westerns for me to preview FREE for 10 days. If I decide to keep them, I'll pay for just 4 of the books at the low subscriber price of $2.75 each; a total $11.00 (a $21.00 value). Then each month I'll receive the 6 newest and best Westerns to preview Free for 10 days. If I'm not satisfied I may return them within 10 days and owe nothing. Otherwise I'll be billed at the special low subscriber rate of $2.75 each; a total of $16.50 (at least a $21.00 value) and save $4.50 off the publishers price. There are never any shipping, handling or other hidden charges. I understand I am under no obligation to purchase any number of books and I can cancel my subscription at any time, no questions asked. In any case the 2 FREE books are mine to keep.

Name _____

Street Address _____ Apt. No. _____

City _____ State _____ Zip Code _____

Telephone _____

Signature _____
(if under 18 parent or guardian must sign)

Terms and prices subject to change. Orders subject to acceptance by True Value Home Subscription Services, Inc.

11478-2

J. R. ROBERTS

THE GUNSMITH

__THE GUNSMITH #1: MACKLIN'S WOMEN	0-515-10145-1/$3.99
__THE GUNSMITH #136: VALLEY MASSACRE	0-515-11084-1/$3.99
__THE GUNSMITH #137: NEVADA GUNS	0-515-11105-8/$3.99
__THE GUNSMITH #139: VIGILANTE HUNT	0-515-11138-4/$3.99
__THE GUNSMITH #140: SAMURAI HUNT	0-515-11168-6/$3.99
__THE GUNSMITH #141: GAMBLER'S BLOOD	0-515-11196-1/$3.99
__THE GUNSMITH #142: WYOMING JUSTICE	0-515-11218-6/$3.99
__GUNSMITH GIANT : TROUBLE IN TOMBSTONE	0-515-11212-7/$4.50
__THE GUNSMITH #143: GILA RIVER CROSSING	0-515-11240-2/$3.99
__THE GUNSMITH #145: GILLETT'S RANGERS	0-515-11285-2/$3.99
__THE GUNSMITH #146: RETURN TO DEADWOOD	0-515-11315-8/$3.99
__THE GUNSMITH #147: BLIND JUSTICE	0-515-11340-9/$3.99
__THE GUNSMITH #148: AMBUSH MOON	0-515-11358-1/$3.99
__THE GUNSMITH #149: SPANISH GOLD	0-515-11377-8/$3.99
__THE GUNSMITH #150: THE NIGHT OF THE WOLF	0-515-11393-X/$3.99
__THE GUNSMITH #151: CHAMPION WITH A GUN	0-515-11409-X/$3.99
__THE GUNSMITH #152: LETHAL LADIES	0-515-11437-5/$3.99
__THE GUNSMITH #153: TOLLIVER'S DEPUTIES	0-515-11456-1/$3.99
__THE GUNSMITH #154: ORPHAN TRAIN	0-515-11478-2/$3.99
__THE GUNSMITH #155: THE MAGICIAN (NOV)	0-515-11495-2/$3.99

Payable in U.S. funds. No cash orders accepted. Postage & handling: $1.75 for one book, 75¢ for each additional. Maximum postage $5.50. Prices, postage and handling charges may change without notice. Visa, Amex, MasterCard call 1-800-788-6262, ext. 1, refer to ad # 206d

Or, check above books Bill my: ☐ Visa ☐ MasterCard ☐ Amex
and send this order form to:
The Berkley Publishing Group Card#_____ (expires)
390 Murray Hill Pkwy., Dept. B   ($15 minimum)
East Rutherford, NJ 07073   Signature_____
Please allow 6 weeks for delivery.   Or enclosed is my: ☐ check ☐ money order

Name_____ Book Total $_____

Address_____ Postage & Handling $_____

City_____ Applicable Sales Tax $_____
                                                        (NY, NJ, PA, CA, GST Can.)
State/ZIP_____ Total Amount Due $_____

THE GUNSMITH

There's not much one man can do against a dozen outlaws—unless that one man is the Gunsmith. When Clint Adams runs across a gang of Comancheros ambushing a small wagon train, he heads for cover and sets up a hail of lead that makes the bushwhackers think they're outgunned.

When the smoke clears and the outlaws turn tail, Clint finds himself saddled with a responsibility he never wanted. The convoy he saved is a wagon train of twenty children—orphans setting out for a new life in California—and his conscience won't let him abandon them. Thanks to his sense of duty, Clint's got an outlaw gang on his trail and, just maybe, a jail term for kidnapping...if he lives long enough!

OVER FIVE MILLION GUNSMITH BOOKS IN PRINT!